the bronze claws

An Inner Sanctum Mystery

PAUL KRUGER

Sebenthall, R E

SIMON AND SCHUSTER

NEW YORK

First printing
SBN 671-21155-2
Library of Congress Catalog Card Number: 74-179583
Designed by Jack Jaget
Manufactured in the United States of America
By The Book Press, Brattleboro, Vt.

THE
BRONZE
CLAWS

1

"BRACE YOURSELF," Mickey, my secretary, admonished me as she walked into my office with the morning mail. "The Mad Poet has struck again."

I'd been buried in the Emerson estate since eight o'clock. A real headache. Half a million dollars, thirteen heirs, including a pet Persian cat named Nightingale, most of the heirs mad at each other and threatening to sue for justice, all of them mad at Nightingale. The only one of the bunch who hadn't been storming into the office regularly to raise a little hell was Nightingale. Good old Nightingale.

I leaned back, glad of a breather, and took the envelope Mickey handed me. It was addressed to me personally as the others had been with a heavy black marking pen and bore an Astoria postmark. Mickey had already slit it open. I extracted the sheet of typing paper. The message was printed in large black letters.

> Here's the castle,
> look inside.
> Somebody killed,
> somebody lied.

"Fascinating," I observed. "I mean, the guy doesn't get any better, does he? Just assuming it is a he. But he does get a little more explicit."

"You can say that again. Now somebody's killed—that's explicit, all right. I'm beginning to wonder, Phil. *Is* this just some jokester? I mean, the first time it looked that way, sure. But this is the third time."

It was indeed. The first message had arrived six weeks ago. Same kind of ordinary envelope, same paper and printing. That one had read:

> Here's the castle,
> open the door,
> walk inside.
> There's plenty more.

Three weeks later we had been honored with another stanza. That too had been slightly more explicit than the first.

> Here's the castle,
> study the scene.
> Things are not
> the way they seem.

I opened my desk drawer, took out the envelope in which the other two stanzas reposed. I examined them again, shook my head. "It's got to be some kook with a slightly sick sense of humor, Mickey."

"But who'd bother to keep up a silly prank over such a period of time? I don't know, Phil." Her face was dubious. "Maybe you should take these to the police."

I winced. "Can't you just hear the riotous guffaws of my good friend Lieutenant Jerry Howe?"

"Why should you care? Let him have his laugh. Afterwards he might get down to business about them."

"And do what? Check for fingerprints that wouldn't be there or wouldn't tell us anything even if they were there? Find a castle? Find a poet? I tell you it's got to be some screwball. Unless . . ."

"Unless what?"

I shoveled the latest missive into the envelope with the others. "I wouldn't," I said grimly, "put it past that mutton-head Jerry Howe to be pulling this himself. And just waiting to give me the horse laugh when I come panting down to headquarters."

"Well, I don't think it's a very funny subject if it's the subject I think it is," Mickey said darkly and went away.

I went through the rest of the mail. Most of it concerned the far-flung Emerson holdings. I put it all aside for the moment and chewed my pencil. Then I leaned over to the intercom.

"Lee here yet?" Lee is my law partner, senior member.

"Yes, he just came in," Mickey said.

I retrieved the Mad Poet file from my desk drawer and repaired to Lee's cubicle. He was unloading his attaché case onto the desk. He looked glum. All very routine, of course. Perhaps a quarrel with Doris, his wife. Perhaps— Then I noticed his pipe, clenched in a corner of his mouth, bowl upside down. That was a very bad sign. It could mean he had quit smoking.

As if we didn't have trouble enough. Nightingale and the Emerson tribe, a Mad Poet sending mysterious messages, and now this.

I cleared my throat carefully. "Uh—everything okay?"

"Did I say it wasn't?" he demanded ominously.

"No, I just meant . . ."

He flung down the empty case and yanked his chair around, sank into it, jerked the pipe from his mouth, looked at it bitterly and thrust it into a drawer. "What's eating you?"

"I have a feeling this isn't the time to bring it up," I said, "but we have received another of those crank letters—if crank letters they be."

"We have?" He began to paw through the stuff on his desk. "And what does this one say?"

I read it to him. He went on shuffling sheafs of paper and did not comment. Finally I ventured, "Well, what do you think? I'm beginning to wonder if I shouldn't take these to the police."

He stopped shuffling papers and looked at me. "I would like to point out one thing, if I may. These abominations have been addressed not to this firm, but to you personally. Right?"

"Well, yes, in a manner of speaking. That is, the firm name is there under my name. Still, I suppose—"

"Exactly. Some idiot who knows you as a result of some of the deplorable publicity you have brought upon this firm has chosen to correspond with you in this—this miserable doggerel. Very well. They are *your* letters, and they are *your* problem. So why bother me with them?"

I sighed. "It was thoughtless of me. Well, I'll just get along." I got as far as the door and looked back. "Oh, by the way. You haven't, by any chance—uh—quit smoking, have you?"

He raised an eyebrow. "Did I say I had?"

"No, but—"

"Well, when I've quit smoking I'll let you know," he snarled. "Is that clear?"

"Of course, of course."

I backed out hastily and got to Mickey's desk, where she was typing away. I leaned over and whispered. "I think he's quit smoking. He isn't admitting it yet, but all the usual signs are there."

Her hands fell from the keys and she looked up in dismay. "What'll we do? I'd rather go over to the zoo and crawl in with Googoo the gorilla."

"Me, too. But courage, Mrs. Whipperfurth." She had recently and needlessly gone and gotten herself married. "It can't last more than a few days."

"A *few* days!" she wailed.

"I know, I know—each day a year. Nevertheless, courage. We'll see it through together." I patted her shoulder and went back to my office, where I retired the Mad Poet file. Then I phoned Doris.

"He's quit smoking," I said.

"I'm afraid so, Phil. Of course, I'd be glad if I thought he'd really give it up. But we'll all go through this agony and then he'll break down."

"How did it happen?"

"It was a TV commercial last night—the one that says don't fool yourself that smoking a pipe or cigars is any less dangerous than smoking cigarettes."

"Yes, I've seen it," I said. "It's a real killer."

"I don't mind so much for myself," she said bravely. "It's the children."

"I know. They won't understand when he starts cracking up. Well, listen, we'll keep in touch. And meanwhile just carry on as best we can."

I hung up and tackled the pile of mail again. The Emerson estate was a juicy piece of business for us, but it had been taking my prime time for a month now and I realized I was beginning to welcome distractions—even mad poets and castles.

I welcomed it when, ten minutes later, Mickey tapped and stepped inside.

"There's a lady here to see you."

"Well, I need something to cheer me up. A young lady?"

"Yes, and with—" she made vague motions—"lots of goodies. She'll cheer you up, I'm sure of it. But what about me?"

"Perhaps a handsome young man will come along." I paused and frowned. "But no, that's out. You had to go and get married, didn't you?"

"Yes, and the way things seem to be going around here I may just decide to go home and be a housewife." She opened the door and put her head out. "Mr. Kramer will see you, Miss Wood."

2

WHEN FATE knocks it is apt to do so very simply and unob-
trusively. It takes you a while to realize that it *has* knocked.
In this case it took me almost as long as it took Miss Wood
to cross the room to my desk. I was waiting with out-
stretched hand and the usual serviceable banalities.

"Very nice to meet you, Miss Wood. Please sit down—
right here."

She did so, moving with a graceful leisure that was lovely
to behold. I was so busy beholding that I almost fell over
the corner of the desk as I worked my way back to my chair.

"It's very good of you to see me without an appointment,
Mr. Kramer. Naturally I would have called for one, but I
just flew in from New York and I am in something of a
hurry."

Sleek legs being crossed, and mini-skirt sliding a little
higher over panty-hosed thighs. Huge white purse being
deposited beside her chair. Kramer's attention riveted.

"My name," she said, "is Holly Wood."

"You wouldn't be kidding?" I asked doubtfully.

"Not at all. This is the kind of grisly thing parents do to

children, then wonder why their children end up on pot in the East Village."

"True," I conceded. "Still—look what Wolfgang Amadeus Mozart's parents named him, and he didn't end up on pot in the East Village." I paused, leaning forward, the better to garner details. She was probably in her mid-twenties. Her eyes were an incredible cornflower blue. Her hair was auburn, worn short and helmetlike. Her cleavage was startling. "But actually—did you?"

"For a while, yes. Long enough to find out I had some establishment tastes I couldn't shake. Like ice cubes and hot showers and clean sheets. So . . ."

"So you split."

"Finally, yes. Back to the establishment. Back to nine to five." She stirred—and a lovely perfume stirred with her, and so did my senses. "Perhaps the truth is that my parents died a long time ago and if you don't have parents to rebel against, the rebellion fizzles out in fairly short order. Anyway—" She broke off, shrugged, cast me an enchanting little smile. "This isn't getting to business, is it?"

"No," I sighed. "So if we must, how can I help you, Miss Wood?"

"I'm looking for a man," she said. "In fact, I'm looking for two men. I'm hoping you can help me find them."

It was a depressing start. But I nodded encouragingly. "Two men. I see. Well, tell me a little more about this."

"Of course. The first man disappeared three years ago. He was—is—my brother. At least, I have to hope it's a case of is. But I don't know. So that's why I'm here."

I drew a quiet little breath of relief. Only a brother after all. "You have reason to believe he might be here in Astoria, Miss Wood? Or in this vicinity?"

"Yes. But let me explain a little more fully. Ted and I

were the only children of my parents, and despite the fact
that he was five years older than I we were always quite
close, especially after Mother and Father died. There was a
little family money, and we both came into our share at
twenty-one. Ted had hippie leanings and the moment he
collected his inheritance he split for San Francisco and the
Haight-Ashbury scene. That was about six years ago."

She leaned down to open the white purse.

"Cigarette?" I asked alertly. "Try one of mine."

"Oh, thank you—"

She accepted the one I proffered and leaned over to my
cigarette lighter. The perfume wafted up from her auburn
hair . . . La Dangerous, La Trouble . . . something deadly
like that. My gaze slid to her cleavage. La Temptation.
Then she drew back.

"Thank you," she said.

"Thank *you*," I murmured.

She let that pass with a faint demure smile. "To get on
with my story. I heard from Ted occasionally during those
next few years and finally received a letter that told me he
was in Denver. That would have been about four years ago.
He was working, he said—actually working, which meant
he'd run through his money, of course. Unfortunately he
didn't tell me what he was doing. Then a year later I had
a letter sent from here, from Astoria. In it he said he was
leaving to go back to S.F."

She paused, blew smoke. "And that was the last I heard
from Ted. Eventually I began to grow concerned about his
silence. I contacted a friend of his in S.F., who made queries
among other friends and learned that Ted had apparently
never returned to S.F. So, as far as I know, he is still in this
vicinity."

I nodded. "It's possible, though three years is a long

time and I suppose he might have gone somewhere else."

"Oh, I realize that. But I've grown more and more concerned, Mr. Kramer, and finally I felt I had to make some attempt to find him. I didn't know where else to start but here. I also realized—" She stopped, nibbled her underlip hesitantly. "Well, I realized that Ted might be in trouble of some sort. That's why I did what I did. I went to a private investigator."

"How long ago was this?"

"Six weeks ago. He wasn't much of a private investigator," she admitted. "But I wanted the type of man he seemed to be. Someone, that is, who would just try to find Ted for me and not concern himself about the, well, shall I say the ethical aspects of the matter, if it turned out that Ted was in trouble or even—" she hesitated again—"even in hiding. You understand what I mean?"

"I understand. But was Ted prone to the sort of trouble you seem to have in mind—serious trouble, let's say?"

"No, he wasn't. But it has been a long time since I've seen him or know anything about the kind of life he was leading. And after his money ran out—well, who knows? To be honest, though, I'm only thinking in terms of trouble because I can't conceive of any other explanation for his long silence. Except, of course—" her voice faltered slightly —"the possibility that he's dead."

"Well, that's the remotest possibility of all," I said. "So let's not worry ourselves about it yet. To return to this private eye . . ."

"Yes. Well, he had this dinky little East Village office and he was a kind of a dinky little man called Ben Manning. I gave him five hundred expense money, plus the flight money, to come out here and look for Ted."

"Let's see if I can guess what happened," I said. "He never came back—which is why you're looking for two men."

She nodded miserably. "That's exactly it. After a couple of weeks in which I'd heard nothing from him I started phoning his office. He had no residential address listed, so I suppose he shared a pad in the East Village with someone or maybe even slept and lived in that office. Anyway, I never got an answer. And finally when I tried to call that number I was told service had been cut off. I went around there and rounded up another tenant, who said he'd been evicted for not paying his rent and they had sold the stuff in his office. Apparently he had never returned to New York at all. I didn't know how to find anyone who might actually have known Manning, so it was a dead end."

I leaned back in my chair. "You're aware of the obvious explanation? That he simply absconded with your money?"

"Yes, I know that's possible. But I can't be sure. And I'd like to be sure. Along, of course, with trying to find Ted myself." She paused, her face tightening with anxiety. "When all's said and done, that dinky little man worries me. What if he really did try to find Ted and—and got into something he couldn't handle? What if he's dead because he tried to help me? It would be my fault. I feel responsible, Mr. Kramer—I really do."

I regarded her in silence for a moment. It was very difficult to regard her and keep your mind on anything else. "Miss Wood," I said sternly. "I get the feeling you're not leveling with me. I get the feeling you have good reason to think your brother *is* in serious trouble, or you wouldn't be jumping to the conclusion that this private eye might be dead as a result of trying to find him."

"That's not true, Mr. Kramer," she said earnestly. "But I'm afraid I've worried about the whole thing so much and for so long that I've begun to—well, exaggerate things out of all proportion. That's understandable, isn't it?"

"Yes, I suppose so. Still, if you've come here to ask me to try to find these men, and I assume that's your purpose, I'm obliged to point out that the police can give you far more help than I can. And I think you should go to them."

She shook her head slowly. "No fuzz. That's absolutely out. If Ted is here and in trouble I'm not going to risk setting the fuzz on him. I mean—well, not unless I have to, not unless there's no other way." She sat there, looking crushed for a moment. Then she raised the lovely blue gaze directly to mine. "You won't consider helping me, then?" she asked mournfully.

"No, I—" I stopped. "That is—well, I—"

Her face lit up instantly. "Look, I'm really not asking very much," she exclaimed eagerly. "I have a week to try to get a look at the scene. I know Ted will be hanging out with hippies if he's here—and since Manning knew that, he certainly went among the hippies, too. But where do I find the hippies? Don't you see? I need someone who knows this town to help me. And . . ." She reached down, hauled the big white purse onto her lap, opened it, extracted a fat bill-fold. "I'm willing to pay anything. Would a thousand-dollar retainer do, Mr. Kramer? If not, just tell me what would do."

La Temptation . . . I sat there and mulled it. Lee would blow a fuse, of course. And I still had a rather uneasy feeling she wasn't leveling with me. Nevertheless, I'd been working too hard, hadn't I? I needed a change from the Emerson tribe and the Emerson squabbles. I needed a rest

—a short, well-financed rest. And what better time to take it than while Lee was in the throes of nicotine withdrawal?

"It is possible," I said, "that a thousand-dollar retainer would help me convince my partner that I should put other things aside for a few days."

She was already counting it out, long elegant fingers moving swiftly and expertly to deposit twenty fifties on my desk. I scooped them up and looked at her. "You understand I can't guarantee success," I stipulated. "And that if we run into something that in my opinion calls for the fuzz I'll call the fuzz."

She nodded. "That's fair enough."

I reached for an envelope, stuffed the money into it, scribbled a message for Lee on it. "Now—can you describe Ben Manning? I think the best way to start is by trying to trace him. It will be a fresher trail—assuming, of course, that he really did make efforts to find your brother."

"He was a small man," she said. "Five-six probably, thin wiry type. Thirty-five, forty, I'd say. Dark hair, mustache. Brown eyes, and he wore big pink shades—you know the kind they wear nowadays."

I jotted it down on a pad. "If he was the kind of shoestring operator you've indicated and not overloaded with expense money he probably stayed at some second-class hotel near the hippie area. We'll check out those places. But first I phone the fuzz."

Alarm leaped into her face. "I thought we—"

"Relax. This won't tell them a thing, but may tell us something that would save us a lot of trouble." I reached for the phone and got Lieutenant Jerry Howe at Homicide. "Phil, Jerry. I need some information. I want to know if a man answering this description has been picked up by police here for any reason or brought into the morgue in the last six weeks. I don't have a name, just this description." I read it off.

"That'll take some checking," Jerry groused. "What's it all about?"

"Confidential, to protect my client. Unless we get a yes on either question."

"Okay, I'll see what I can find out."

I hung up, shoved all the Emerson papers back into the folders, stacked them neatly for Mickey to file. Maybe the whole mess would go away before I had to tackle it again.

"All set, Miss Wood," I said and rose.

Mickey looked up inquiringly as we reached the reception room.

"I've been summoned away on business," I said. "May be gone the rest of the day. As soon as I'm out the door you take this in to Lee and tell him."

I tried to hand her the envelope with the money in it, but she pulled back. "I wouldn't go in there for—"

"Somebody has to."

"But why me?"

"Because he won't hit a woman." I leaned down and whispered. "There's a thousand-dollar retainer in that envelope."

"Oh—well, that's different. Should help, huh?"

"Should help," I agreed, and steered Holly Wood out the door.

3

SHE HAD a gold Mustang in the building parking lot. "I rented it at the airport and took my luggage to a motel—the High Tor," she said. "That's where I heard about you."

"How?"

"Just asked the clerk for the name of a good attorney."

"I'm honored. But what's the sense of running up mileage on a rented car when we can take mine?"

She agreed there was no sense in it. I helped her into my bus and headed over to the Spaight Street district. The last four, five years have seen a steady influx of hippies into that area, which had been seedy enough at best. There were probably half a dozen shabby hotels we could try there with an even chance of hitting Ben Manning's trail. I explained this to her, adding, "There's another place I've got in mind if we don't hit pay dirt around here. A hippie commune up in the hills south of here, a place called Cricket Town."

"That sounds interesting. Have you ever been there?"

"No, but I like to look in on how the other half lives, so I wouldn't mind if we have to check it out. By the way, do you have a picture of Ted?"

"No, I gave the only one I had to Manning. But I can describe him."

"Shoot."

"Six feet, brown hair, hazel eyes, rather heavyset. In the picture he sent me, and that was apparently taken while he was working in Denver, he was wearing his hair short and had shaved off his beard."

"Any distinguishing marks or features that might help?"

"No, I'm afraid not."

It took us half an hour to check out three small hotels just off or on Spaight Street. The fourth, the Trenton House, was a cut above the other places; old, but still trying earnestly to preserve appearances. We threaded through the potted palms and the cigar-chewing regulars to the desk. The clerk was trying, too; he was neat and polite. His gaze narrowed when I told him what we wanted.

"Just a minute—" He went away to examine a file on the desk behind him, then came back with a card in his hand. "I thought I recognized the name. We have it here. A Ben Manning skipped out without paying his bill. He was here from June 13 to June 23."

Holly Wood's eyes met mine. "That would be about right," she said. "He left on the twelfth, or was supposed to."

"You impounded his belongings?" I asked the clerk.

"Certainly. He had registered with a New York City address. We sent a bill there, got no response. So his stuff is probably still in the basement. As I remember, it didn't amount to much. A couple of cheap bags."

"We'll pay the bill and take the bags," I said. "I'm his brother and—"

He shrugged, indicating it wasn't necessary to provide a

story. "Sure. I'll have a boy bring them up and you can sign a receipt for them."

While we waited I settled the bill and quizzed him, but learned little. So far as he knew, Manning had made no long-distance calls or received any. He had had no visitors. He, the clerk, had not been on duty the last time Manning left his key at the desk, so of course had no idea where he was going or why he had failed to return. The one thing he did remember was that several days earlier Manning had asked him directions for finding a hippie joint called the Lost Cause.

"Where *do* you find it?" I asked.

"Over on Cherokee Street, nine-hundred block."

A boy came with the bags and I signed the receipt as George Manning, brother. Not that anybody cared.

"You have a nice flair for it," Holly Wood commented as we headed back to the car.

"For what?"

"Petty deceit—one of the establishment virtues, of course."

"Now, wait a minute," I said. "Just because I'm almost thirty no fresh ex–flower child is going to talk to me thata-way."

"I'm sorry," she said contritely. "Honestly I am. I'm so used to thinking and spouting in those grooves that I find myself still doing it at times. Believe me when I say that I'm trying to mature."

I gazed at her thoughtfully. "Believe me, in some ways you have succeeded admirably," I murmured.

"So we are friends again?"

"Until I can talk you into something better, yes."

As soon as we got to the car I opened the bags. The loot

was disappointing. A couple of dirty shirts, extra slacks, underwear, turtleneck sweater, toothbrush, a bottle of pills, a pair of old shoes. If he'd had an electric razor, and he no doubt had, the flunky who'd cleaned up his room had helped himself to it. A couple of paperbacks were stuck in the flap of the cover of one bag. *I Was a Teen-aged Lesbian* and *A Handbook of Astrology.*

"Hmmm, our friend had esoteric tastes," I observed.

I shook both books, and a scrap of cardboard floated out of one. It was half the flap of a matchbook from Corky's Pizza Palace. On the back of it was scribbled: *"Denver Post,* July 15, 1968."

"That's interesting," I said. "I'm in favor of repairing to the public library and trying to learn why Ben Manning was interested in this particular copy of a Denver paper."

I piled things back into the bags and retired them to the car trunk. Then we headed over to the main library. It had *Denver Post* files, of course, and a personable maiden conducted us to a reading room and produced the issue of Monday, July 15, 1968.

"Please handle with care," she advised.

I started, with care, on page one. It had been a day like any other day. War, murder, traffic accidents, price hikes, City Hall skullduggery. But at the bottom under a modest headline I found a slightly more interesting item.

> The body of Dr. David Castle, 44, well-known Denver physician, was found early yesterday, badly burned, in the smoldering ruins of his isolated mountain cabin near Piñon Point.
>
> Dr. Castle had been spending the weekend alone at the cabin. The Sheriff's office at West Bend stated that the fire

had apparently started late Saturday night but had not been discovered until dawn Sunday. It is believed that it may have been caused by the explosion of a gasoline lamp. The body was burned beyond recognition and has been turned over to the state crime laboratory for positive identification.

Dr. Castle is survived by his wife, Mavis, 1143 Winslow Drive, and by a half brother, Rufus Langley, of Astoria.

I went on staring at the item while something tried to surface in my mind. Castle . . . Had I heard the name before, or— Then it floated up. The Mad Poet. *Here's the castle, look inside. Somebody killed, somebody lied.*

"What is it?" Holly stage-whispered.

I pushed the paper over to her. "Read this."

She did so and raised puzzled eyes. "It means something?"

"It just might. First of all, it could tie in with some peculiar anonymous messages I've been receiving at the office." I told her about that. "Farfetched perhaps, but just possibly someone was trying to steer me to this matter of a doctor named Castle dying in a fire. Don't ask me why. I don't know why. But add to it that Ben Manning had some reason to be interested in this particular copy of the *Post* and—" I broke off. "All right. Better not go off half cocked. So hold everything while I go through the whole paper."

I did that very carefully and found nothing at all that struck me as likely to account for Ben Manning's concern with this particular issue. I summoned the personable maiden and asked if we could have the next five issues of the *Post,* and they were duly brought. On the seventeenth there was a second-page story to the effect that the body of Dr. Castle had been identified by means of various personal belongings, watch, ring, keys. Funeral services had been set and so on. End of the affair. Nothing appeared in the later copies.

"I thought they could make identifications by teeth," Holly said when I'd pushed it over for her perusal.

"True, but since the point isn't even mentioned here it's possible the good doctor wore plastic dentures. Good hot fire, goodbye plastic dentures." I thought a minute. "You never knew what Ted was working at in Denver?"

"No."

"But that letter you received three years ago from Astoria was dated when?"

"I don't remember the exact date and I didn't keep it, not realizing I might need it someday. I'd say it was dated early in July."

"That makes it the same month in which this happened."

"Yes," she said slowly. "But—so what?"

"Darned if I know myself at this point, Holly. I just have a feeling that we should dig a little further on this." I tapped the paper. "Suppose we run up to Denver and do a bit of snooping. We can pick up some lunch on the way. Okay?"

"What about this place, the Lost Cause, that Manning had asked about at the hotel?"

"We'll look in there when we get back."

She gathered up the big white purse. "You're the tour director. Let's go."

4

WE HAD LUNCH on the outskirts of Denver—shrimp salad for Holly, chili and a sandwich for me. While she finished off with a second cup of coffee I repaired to the phone booth and put in a call for my old friend Knox Norton at the *Post*.

"Sure, I remember that case, Phil. In fact, I knew Castle, he treated me for asthma for a couple of years. He was a damned good doctor—when he was sober."

"Like that, huh?"

"Yes, an alcoholic. He was still on a hospital staff here and getting by, but it was probably only a matter of time. Reason he had this cabin, it was a place he could go for weekend drunks. Pretty well-known fact. So nobody was too surprised when the place burned down. Consensus was he accidentally set fire to something in the cabin and was too stoned to get out."

"The means of identification seem poor."

"Right. More a case of nothing to prove it wasn't him. But you know how insurance companies dig, and eventually they must have been satisfied, because the widow collected five hundred thousand double indemnity on accidental death."

I whistled. "She did, did she? Any suspicion of foul play?"

"Plenty of suspicion, but it all came to nothing. Mrs. Castle was—is—a very attractive woman and she had a boy friend, Leslie Rainier, who runs a small ad agency here, Rainier and Marking. Nobody blamed her much, you understand, because along with being a drunk Castle was a skirt-chaser. Anyway, widow and boy friend got checked out thoroughly, you may be sure. And both had cast-iron alibis for the night of the fire."

"Anybody else involved—like other relatives, or lady friends?"

"Castle did have a half brother, Rufus Langley. But he was severely injured in an auto accident some years back—there was brain damage, and he never made a full recovery. I think he's still hospitalized somewhere. As for lady friends, no one I can name."

"Did Mrs. Castle remarry?"

"No. She sold the Castle place and moved into an apartment, and that's about the last I heard of her."

"Did Castle have his own offices or was he in with associates?"

"He was in with Rudy Watson for years."

"He might be a good one to talk to."

"Sure, except that he died last year. But wait. His son took over his practice and they have a nurse up there who dates back to Castle's time. In fact, she was Castle's office nurse for years. Her name is Parker—Irene Parker. Now, *she* might be a good one to talk to. That would be Watson and Braddock, in the Medical Arts Building. You wouldn't care to tell me what you're up to, Phil?"

"You can be sure I will if anything exciting develops," I said.

We drove around to the Medical Arts Building, and the elevator whisked us to the fourteenth floor and a severely modern reception room behind the door marked "Watson and Braddock."

"We would like to see Miss Irene Parker," I informed the lady at the desk.

"You have an appointment with one of our doctors?"

"No, we just want to see Miss Parker. A personal matter, quite urgent. I'm an attorney. Perhaps you would give her my card."

It all seemed to be highly unorthodox, but she took the card and vanished through a door at the rear of the room. Presently she reappeared and held the door aside for us. "Miss Parker will give you a few minutes."

The room was small, stuffed with filing cabinets and the desk at which Miss Parker sat. She rose as we entered. A big heavyset woman, perhaps in her late thirties or early forties, with a face as hard and starched as her uniform.

"You wished to see me?"

"Yes. I'm Phil Kramer, Miss Parker. This is Miss Wood, a client of mine. We've learned that you were once Dr. David Castle's office nurse."

"That is correct." Her eyes were really pretty, I decided —large and blue-green, fringed with very dark lashes—but the coldly steady way she had of staring straight at you could easily keep you from noticing it. "What about it?" she added.

"We are looking for a man named Ted Wood, Miss Parker, and we think he might have been known to Dr. Castle. Perhaps as a patient or—"

She broke in crisply. "Ted Wood? Well, of course. Dr. Castle once employed a man called Ted Wood. He worked at his home, handyman, yardman—that sort of thing. Something happened, I'm not sure I remember just what, but I believe it concerned some missing money. Rightly or wrongly, Dr. Castle suspected this man of having taken the money and fired him."

"This was when, Miss Parker?"

She thought a moment. "Perhaps three or four months before Dr. Castle died, which would make it—let's see, sometime in the early spring of 'sixty-eight."

"How long had he worked for Dr. Castle?"

"Oh, that's hard to remember. I'd say probably close to a year."

"You wouldn't know what happened to Ted Wood afterwards? Where he went, so on?"

"Under the circumstances, I doubt David ever knew—or cared." She frowned in an annoyed way for the "David" that had slipped out inadvertently. "May I ask why you are concerned about this man?"

"He seems to have vanished, Miss Parker, just about the time that Dr. Castle died."

"Really?" She shrugged before adding, "Well, he seemed very much a drifter, so that's probably not surprising."

"You knew him?"

"Not really. I did see him a time or two when he came here to the office on errands for Dr. Castle. But I gathered from Dr. Castle's remarks about him that he was lazy and unreliable. A hippie type, apparently. If help of that kind hadn't been so hard to get I doubt Dav—Dr. Castle would have kept him on as long as he did."

"You say he was a hippie type. Long-haired, bearded?"

She looked faintly horrified. "Indeed not—not while he worked for Dr. Castle. Dr. Castle would not have tolerated that."

"If I might ask another question, has a private detective named Ben Manning ever come here to question you?"

"My good man," she said grimly. "After Dr. Castle died so many detectives—investigators, whatever you call them—came to talk to me that—"

"No, I mean just lately, Miss Parker. Say within the last six weeks."

She stared. "But it was all over long ago. Why would anyone come asking me questions now?"

"This man would have been looking for Ted Wood, as we are," I said.

"Oh, I see." She shook her head. "In any case, no—no one has come here with questions of any kind in a long long time." She paused. "You didn't really answer my question as to why you are looking for Ted Wood."

I glanced at Holly, indicating it was up to her.

"Ted is my brother, Miss Parker," she said. "It's been three years since I've seen or heard from him and I have grown alarmed about him. The last I did hear he was in this area, so I have asked Mr. Kramer to try to help me find him."

Irene Parker gave her that long unnerving steady stare. It managed to convey the impression that such a brother was a misfortune and any hunt for such a brother a folly beyond words.

"One more thing, Miss Parker," I said. "Dr. Castle has a half brother, I believe."

"Yes, he's been in a mental sanitarium for years, following brain injury in an auto accident."

"Around here?"

"Down at Astoria. The Four Pines. You probably know of it. A very expensive place."

"Is he completely non compos?"

"No, merely given to various harmless delusions." Irene Parker looked at her watch. "I'm sorry, but Dr. Watson is due back from lunch at any moment and I have things to do."

Since she hadn't asked us to sit down, we didn't have to waste time on getting up. "Thanks very much for seeing us, Miss Parker," I said, and steered Holly toward the door.

We slid downward in the elevator.

"It's a lead of sorts, isn't it?" Holly asked. "Ted did work for this Dr. Castle."

I nodded. "And I think we're justified now in talking to Mrs. Castle. There's a small chance she might know where Ted went after he left them."

I consulted the phone directory in the lobby booth and located Mrs. Mavis Castle at 4224 North Hancock. We got into the car and headed out there. Holly was silent as I maneuvered through traffic.

"What are you thinking?" I asked presently.

She smiled wryly. "That Ted must have been desperate for bread to stay on a job like that for almost a year."

"Maybe it was just a nice easy job. Tell me something. Was Ted on drugs?"

"No. He had a thing about drugs. He believed they were a loser's bag, and of course they are." She paused. "Actually, Ted was a smart boy, Mr. Kramer. If he'd settled down, finished college, gotten started on a career, he could have gone a long way. But he had all these ideas about freedom and self-realization. . . . Well—didn't we all?" she added a little wistfully. "I went through that bit myself, so I know what it's like."

I braked for a light. "But you outgrew it."

"I suppose that's what you'd call it. At least, I began to see it for a dead end. I began to see that the only real freedom in the world is in having choices. And believe me, you don't have any choices at all holed up in a rat-infested loft, scrounging for spaghetti and speed with a bunch of mind-blown kids. It's just one long trip to nowhere."

"Maybe Ted eventually outgrew that scene, too. Do you suppose he might have?"

She considered it for a moment. "It's possible, I suppose. Still, the last I heard he was going back to Haight-Ashbury, and that sure doesn't sound like it."

"But he apparently didn't go back." I paused. "Could he have been deliberately misleading you when he told you that?"

She turned to look at me. "But why would he want to mislead me?"

"Darned if I know. It's just a stray thought. Only it occurred to me that if he had tired of the hippie scene we could be barking up the wrong trees."

"Well . . ." She looked unhappy. "We don't know what else to do, do we?"

"Nope. Anyway, we've got this much of a lead, so let's see where it goes. Oh, by the way—"

"Yes?"

"We've known each other for several hours and you're still calling me Mr. Kramer. Can't we do something about that?"

I got a cryptic little smile for my effort. "Certainly—Counselor."

"That's not exactly what I had in mind."

"Well, I'm a shy inhibited type. It always takes me twenty-four hours to loosen up enough for a first name. However, since you're being so kind and helpful, I'll try—Phil."

"That's better," I said.

We hit North Hancock at the thirty-hundred block, drifted on to 4224. It was a modest stucco duplex with a fake-Moorish façade and sun-faded awnings.

"Are you sure this is it?" Holly asked dubiously. "I mean, like with five hundred thousand would you be living here?"

"Hmmm, no. I'd be in Bermuda, savoring the tropical fleshpots. But perhaps the widow is a thrifty soul, likes to salt it away and all that good stuff. Anyway, this is it. Wish us luck."

5

THERE WAS no driveway from the street; probably an alley
in back led to garages. I parked at the curb and we walked
up. The unit on the left was Mavis Castle's. The tap-tap of
a typewriter came from an open window. I rang and it
stopped. Presently the inside door behind a screen opened.

She was tall, very slender, with an appealing air of fra-
gility and a preoccupied frown. "Yes?"

"Mrs. Castle?"

"Yes, but I'm terribly busy. If you're selling something—"

"We're not. My name is Phil Kramer. I'm an attorney.
This is Miss Wood, a client. We'd appreciate it if we could
have a few words with you concerning a man who once
worked for you and Dr. Castle."

Her face came alert. "I don't understand."

"Perhaps if we could come in and explain . . . It's quite
important, Mrs. Castle, or we wouldn't be intruding this
way."

The large brown eyes looking at us weren't very good at
deception. Fear flickered in their depths for a moment. But
she got control of it. The shades came down and she was
looking at us with nothing more than a polite wariness.

"Well, if it's important . . . of course." Even her voice had changed, gone flat and remote. She unlatched the screen and stood back. "Come in."

The tiny entry hall opened into a fair-sized living room. She indicated that we could sit down and we took the sofa. While we were doing that she went to a table, got herself a cigarette, lit it, and seated herself in a chair facing us.

I had taken a quick glance around the room. The typewriter we had heard clacking away stood on a desk under a window near the door, a letter or something still rolled into it. The room wasn't unattractive or poorly furnished; half a dozen good, though not new, pieces of furniture may have been leftovers from the Castle home. Certainly the grand piano appeared to be, and the Bokhara rug whose blues and rubies had settled into the beautiful mellowness of age.

The lady wasn't unattractive, either. The big brown eyes and delicately chiseled features gave her too-thin face considerable distinction. Animated it could have been very pretty. But the politely wooden look was still there.

"What was it you wanted to see me about?" she asked.

"A man named Ted Wood who, we understand, once worked for you and Dr. Castle as a handyman, yardman, whatever."

"Yes, a man called Ted Wood once worked for us. What about him?"

"He seems to have disappeared and we are trying to find him, Mrs. Castle. Miss Wood here is his sister and has retained me to help her."

"Disappeared? Ted Wood?" Her brows went up. "Well, he can't have disappeared very far. He must still be around here somewhere, because a man from the Industrial Commission was here, oh, maybe six weeks ago, to inquire about him. He said Ted Wood had put in an injury claim and they were checking into his work record."

Holly's gaze jerked around to meet mine. She looked so startled and hopeful that I hated to put the next question.

"Could you describe this man, Mrs. Castle?" I asked.

"Well, he was quite ordinary. A small man, dark, with a mustache, wearing big tinted glasses."

I looked at Holly. "Would you say that sounded like Ben Manning?"

The hope had faded out of her face. She nodded.

I turned to Mrs. Castle again. "Did he give you his name?"

"It seems as if he did, but I don't recall it. Anyway, I should think if you contacted the Industrial Commission—"

I shook my head. "I'm afraid he was misrepresenting himself, Mrs. Castle. That description you gave me fits a private detective Miss Wood sent here from New York to look for her brother. I might add that this man has vanished, too. He never reported back to Miss Wood, never returned to New York."

There was a long blank silence. Finally she made a small harried gesture with her cigarette. "Well, what is it you want of me, Mr. Kramer? My husband has been dead for three years and Ted Wood left us at least three or four months before he died. Beyond that there isn't a thing I can tell you, and I really do not understand why you have come here."

"That would have been in the spring of 'sixty-eight that Ted Wood left you?"

"Yes."

"There was some trouble over missing money," I said. "And Dr. Castle fired him?"

"How did you know that?" she asked sharply.

"We have already talked to Dr. Castle's office nurse, a Miss Parker."

"I see. Well, we had no real proof it was Ted who had taken the money, but it seemed the only possibility and we didn't want him around with the feeling that we couldn't trust him. So David—Dr. Castle—did discharge him, yes." She paused. It was a rather long silence, as if she were debating whether to say more. Then she said it. "In fairness, I should add that he didn't steal the money. David found it later. He'd tucked it away somewhere in his study and forgotten about it. He—well, he was rather vague about things like that at times. Anyway, David felt very badly about it when he discovered the money and said he was going to try to find Ted and explain."

"Did he do that?"

"I don't know, Mr. Kramer. He contacted the post office and learned that Ted had notified them of a new forwarding address down at Astoria. He told me he intended to try to see Ted there sometime when he went down to visit his brother, who is in an Astoria sanitarium. But whether he actually did I can't say."

"You don't know what that address was, Mrs. Castle?"

She shook her head and turned aside to scrub the cigarette out in a tray on a table. When she looked at us again there was a new if veiled anxiety in her eyes. "When you say Ted Wood has disappeared, exactly what do you mean, Mr. Kramer?"

"I mean that nothing has been heard of him for about three years. He apparently did go down to Astoria, and from there, sometime in July of 'sixty-eight, he wrote a letter to Miss Wood, telling her he intended to return to

San Francisco. Miss Wood contacted friends there later on and learned that he had never done so. In short, so far as she has been able to learn he simply dropped out of sight that summer—just around the time your husband died, Mrs. Castle. Which in itself would have no particular significance, except that—"

The ringing of the doorbell interrupted me. She rose quickly. "Excuse me."

Some women walk, other women have a walk—that is, an exercise in grace. She had a walk, the kind that takes your eyes along. And from the angle at which I was sitting I had a view into the entry hall. I saw her open the door and saw the man step in and automatically reach to embrace her. I saw the look that passed between them, too, as she murmured something to him, probably a quick resumé of the situation. He threw his hat onto a table and followed her into the room. He was fortyish, with dark curly hair graying at the temples, a tanned but rather haggard face, a hard set to the jaw and probing dark eyes.

"This is Mr. Rainier," she said. "Miss Wood, Mr. Kramer. They—they are here to ask some questions about Ted Wood, Les."

So this was the boy friend of old, apparently still on the scene, and apparently as unhappy over us as Mavis Castle had appeared to be.

"What about Ted Wood?" he asked bluntly, having barely acknowledged the introductions.

I explained, and the further I went the more hostile he looked.

"Mavis knows absolutely nothing about this man," he snapped finally. "Why come here?"

"We had hoped she could tell us something."

"Well, she can't. Why don't you go to the Industrial Commission? They were here some weeks ago about him and probably know where he is."

Mavis Castle said, "They don't think that man was from the Industrial Commission, Les. He may have been a private detective employed by Miss Wood to search for her brother."

"And what is more, Mr. Rainier," I threw in, "this detective seems to have disappeared, too. He never reported back to Miss Wood, never returned to New York. We haven't been able to pick up his trail beyond the point where he walked out of an Astoria hotel on the twenty-third of last month—walked out, leaving his luggage and an unpaid bill." I drew the bit of Pizza Palace match folder from my pocket and handed it to Mavis Castle. "We claimed his luggage and found this in it. That, of course is the edition of the *Post* that carried the story concerning your husband's accidental death. Naturally we couldn't help wondering why Manning —the detective—was interested in it."

"What's to prove he wasn't interested in some other item that issue carried?" Rainier demanded.

"In view of everything else, I think it would be too much of a coincidence," I said. "I wonder if you could tell me one thing, Mrs. Castle. Was Ted Wood angry over the fact that your husband fired him? Did he sound off—make threats, anything of that sort?"

She sat down slowly and stared into space for a moment. "Well, he did heatedly deny taking the money, but that was only natural, especially as we know now he didn't take it. But then finally he just shrugged it off in a rather surly way and slammed out of the room. Later that day he packed up and left the house without a word to either of us."

"Turned in keys and such, I suppose?"

"Yes, everything was on the bureau in his room."

"In any case, he had made no threats against Dr. Castle?"

"No."

"Did he know where this mountain cabin was, know that Dr. Castle habitually went up there alone weekends?"

"Yes. David had sent him up there several times to do some work around the place."

Rainier spun around from the window where he'd gone to stand. "What are you getting at with these stupid questions that were asked a dozen times by investigators?"

"I'm getting at the possibility of foul play, which I take it they considered, too, if they asked these same questions."

"Of course they considered it." His voice was harsh and belligerent. "And there was not one iota of evidence to support it. So why should you come here now stirring up fresh trouble?"

"Maybe because several things are apparent now that weren't so apparent at the time," I said. "Mrs. Castle, can you tell me if the investigators made an attempt to find Ted Wood at that time?"

"I don't know," she said. "They did know he had worked here and the circumstances under which he left. They did feel that he might have been angry enough to commit a grudge killing. But just as Les told you, there was absolutely no evidence of foul play. So how far they would have pursued that line of inquiry I can't say."

"And what about the other possibility?" I asked. "Did they consider that?"

Rainier took a step forward, glaring at me. "What other possibility?"

"Les—" Mavis Castle lifted her head wearily. "Please just keep out of it." She turned to me. Her eyes were bright and hot in her pale face, but she spoke very levelly, very calmly. "You're referring to the possibility that my husband did not die in that fire, that he—that he might have used another body?"

From the corner of my eye I caught the swift startled turn of Holly's head. But she didn't speak. And I was intent on the two before me. "Yes, that's about it, Mrs. Castle. Along with the possibility that it was Ted Wood's body he used. Suppose he did go down to Astoria to see Ted as he mentioned wanting to do. Got back on a good footing with him, perhaps gave him some money by way of compensation. Then later, when he needed him, invited him up to the cabin. After all, identification was made on the strength of a number of metal articles, ring, keys, such. Things that could have been planted on another body."

She sat silent, staring down.

"I take it Dr. Castle wore plastic dentures? At least, the newspaper accounts did not mention identification on the basis of teeth. Do you happen to know if Ted Wood wore plastic dentures?"

"I have no idea."

"The insurance investigators were interested in this point, too?"

She nodded. Then she looked up at me. "But—*how?* Suppose it were true. How could David have killed Wood without the cause of death being apparent?"

I shrugged. "Stoned him with drugs or booze, locked him in there so he couldn't escape. It could have been managed, Mrs. Castle. It *has* been managed, and any insurance investigator would know that."

The bright hot eyes were very level on me again. "And why would my husband have done this, Mr. Kramer? Just so *I* could come into all that insurance money?"

"I would guess that you would have been expected to share in due time, Mrs. Castle."

Rainier lunged for me, caught me by the jacket lapel and yanked me to my feet. "You son of a bitch—" he snarled.

"Don't make me punch you, Mr. Rainier," I said coldly. "I'm allowing for your disturbed frame of mind, but if you don't let go fast—"

Mavis Castle had jumped to her feet, too. "Oh, stop it, Les!" she cried. "For heaven's sake, stop it!"

He released me and stepped back, his face working, his fists clenched. "What are you trying to do to her?" he demanded harshly.

"I'm trying to find out what happened to two men," I said. "Ted Wood and Ben Manning. I want to know if they are dead or alive, and if they are dead, why. Polite harmless questions aren't going to get me anything, Mr. Rainier— and you know it as well as I do." I shifted my gaze to Mavis Castle again. "Two years ago you collected five hundred thousand in insurance, Mrs. Castle. Most women would be living high on that. But you are apparently living in a very modest way."

"I—I had debts to pay off," she said desperately. "David had left many debts. And then my father failed in business. He owed a great deal of money. I helped him discharge his obligations."

"Maybe," I said. "Or maybe the money, or a good deal of it anyway, went to your husband."

She stared at me bitterly. "That would be to say that I had been party to an insurance swindle."

"Yes, but possibly an unwitting one at first, Mrs. Castle. Your husband might have proceeded without your knowledge to stage that fire with another body planted in the cabin. And only later let you know that he was alive and wanted part of the insurance money."

I was watching her closely. A pulse had begun to jump in her temple.

"You think I would have—have gone along even then with—with such a terrible thing?" she asked.

"If he threatened, as he may have, to expose the whole thing and accuse you of being an accomplice—yes. What else could you do? Proving you hadn't been an accomplice would have been immensely difficult."

"But that's ridiculous," she said. "To expose it would have been to endanger himself as much as me."

"Not if he were safely out of the country and under good cover. It would have been you who would have had to face the rap."

She whirled away and walked to a window for a moment. Rainier sat slumped in a chair, watching her, obviously restraining himself with an effort. Finally she turned. Her chin was lifted defiantly now and she seemed very calm.

"You've worked out quite a plot there, Mr. Kramer," she said dryly. "All I can do is tell you that you are completely wrong."

I nodded and got to my feet. "I hope I am, Mrs. Castle —I truly do. And if I can find either of the men I'm looking for that will probably prove me wrong. Until then I have to consider all this as at least a remote possibility." I turned to Holly, who had risen, too. "Shall we go?"

Rainier followed us to the door. His anger had subsided, but his face looked drawn and tense.

"Do you think she hasn't been through all this before with police and insurance investigators? If there were a shred of truth to it, they would have found it out."

"Not necessarily," I said. "Not if it were well planned and well executed."

"Dr. Castle would have had no conceivable reason for doing such a thing. He was a successful physician, a well-to-do man."

"That's only half the story," I said. "He was also an alcoholic, close to the skids and probably well aware of it. Maybe a marriage on the rocks, too. You'd know about that, I suppose."

His jaw hardened; he didn't answer.

"Anyway, with plenty of money it wouldn't matter," I said. "He could make himself a new life somewhere else. But he had to have the money. Even half of five hundred thousand could have looked good to him."

"Let her alone—please."

"You're in love with her, aren't you?"

"What if I am?"

"She's been a widow for three years. Why haven't you married her?"

"She'd had enough of marriage—with him."

"Maybe." I opened the door, let Holly precede me through. Then I looked him straight in the eye. "Or maybe, Mr. Rainier, she knows she isn't a widow."

If he had an answer to that I didn't wait for it. We walked down to the curb and got into the car.

"Wow!" Holly said as she settled herself and fished in her bag for cigarettes. "You sure took me by surprise with all that. You can't be serious."

"Why can't I? It's been done, Holly, believe me. It's been done and gotten away with."

"But it means—" She broke off and turned her head

away for a moment as I started the car and slid away from the curb. "It means that Ted is dead, doesn't it?"

"No, even if I'm right that's not a certainty, Holly. Just one possibility."

"But the way it all seems to dovetail—I'm not so sure. He *did* disappear right around that time. And now this whole business of Manning, too. Do you believe their story about him posing as someone from the Industrial Commission?"

"It had the ring of truth and he certainly might have. That doesn't mean they might not have seen through his little ploy—given the fact, of course, that I'm right about the rest of it. Anyway, it does prove one thing we weren't sure about. That Manning did set out to try to find Ted."

We hit the Colfax Avenue intersection and I swung right into heavy after-work traffic. "I think we've done about all we can do here for the present. I'm for getting back and having a go at the Lost Cause. Okay?"

She nodded, and we drove in silence for a while, both of us busy with our thoughts. Then she said, "Do you really believe that if all this is true she was—as you put it—an unwitting accomplice?"

"Just offhand, she didn't strike me as the type who would have coldbloodedly gone along with such a thing in the beginning. How about you?"

"I think I'd agree with that. They seemed—frightened, and yet—" She shook her head a little. "I can't quite get it into words. But returning to Manning. If he figured it as you have and put them on the spot, what do you suppose they would have done?"

"They might have offered to pay him off. Paid him to forget everything, including you."

"But in that case why didn't he return to New York? All he would have had to do was tell me he hadn't been able to learn anything and that would have been the end of it as far as he was concerned."

I nodded. "Which is why I find myself favoring the unpleasant alternative. It would have been cheaper and easier to just kill Manning."

6

It was five-thirty when we got down to Astoria and headed over to Cherokee Street. The Lost Cause was exactly the kind of dump I'd figured it would be: a long narrow hole in the wall, dismally lit, with a beat-up old bar, a scattering of chairs and tables, and a few pop posters tacked up here and there on the walls for décor—or maybe just to hide the worst cracks and peeling paint.

There were a couple of hippies in tribal costume at the far end of the bar and another pair, sex uncertain, at one of the tables. One was reading a book; the one I figured might be a girl was doing things slowly and solemnly with tarot cards. We took bar stools, and the bartender drifted down to us. He had a long horse face framed with long lank hair, and his get-up was straight from Marlboro Country—even to the bandana knotted around his neck. He said, "Yeah, man?" and looked at us from spaniel-sad eyes behind granny glasses. We ordered dry martinis and when he brought them I had a ten-dollar bill in front of me.

"Never mind the change if you can give me a little information," I said.

It didn't cheer him up, but he hunched over on his fore-arms and waited.

"We're looking for a man named Ted Wood," I said.

He studied a poster across the room for a while. "That's funny," he allowed at last.

"Yes? Why?"

"So was some other cat back a while ago."

"How long ago?"

"Maybe a month, six weeks."

"Who did he say he was?"

"He didn't."

"What did he look like?"

"Kind of runty, big shades. Fuzz maybe. You fuzz?"

"No."

He lowered a paw for the bill. My paw got there faster. "You haven't answered the question yet. Do you know this Ted Wood?"

"He split a long time ago, man."

"Then you knew him?"

"Sure. He used to hang around here. Tended bar for me now and then."

"How long ago did he split?"

"Two, three years maybe."

"Could you narrow that down, friend?"

Silence. Thoughts of some kind slopping around behind his sad eyes.

"Well, probably more like three years, man," he said finally.

"Any idea where he went?"

"Nope. He just quit coming in, that's all."

"Did he live around here?"

He looked down at the ten. "That would take another small investment, man."

I reached for my wallet and found a five and put that down on top of the ten.

"He was shacked up with a chick called Viola. She's still around—regular customer. Should be coming in any time now."

"We'd like to talk to her," I said. "And don't tell me it will take another small investment. We'll move over to one of the tables and wait."

He palmed the bills and withdrew. I steered Holly and our drinks over to one of the tables. The martini was awful. I put mine down after one taste and said, "I want to make a phone call, Holly. Keep your eye on things."

The phone was on the wall in a narrow hallway off the back of the room leading to the johns. I fished up a dime and dialed Homicide and caught Jerry Howe just as he was leaving. He had checked out the local supply of recent corpses for me. My description of Ben Manning hadn't rung any bells at the morgue, and the only unidentified body in the last six weeks had been that of a Spanish-American boy knifed in a Spaight Street alley.

"Fill me in on something else," I said. "This hippie commune called Cricket Town. You know where it is?"

"Not exactly, but you could probably find out at Big Rock. It's back in the hills from there."

"Anything you could tell me about it?"

"Not much. A guy called Conrad Baker bought the property and lets this crew of hippies camp out on it. Sheriff down there keeps an eye on it, but so far there hasn't seemed to be any trouble. Why are you interested?"

"Just curious. Thought I'd go have a look at how the other half lives."

"Well, don't forget to wear your love beads," Jerry said and hung up.

By the time I got back to the table there was a new couple at the bar and Spaniel Eyes was talking to the girl. She glanced around at us and I endeavored to look friendly and harmless. She collected a drink and came drifting over with it.

"This on you, man?"

"If you're Viola, sure."

"That's me, man."

She wore jeans, a man's shirt that hung halfway down her thighs, tennis shoes and reddish hair—lots of it.

"Sit down," I said.

She did and, having placed her glass on the table, raised both hands to part the long hair enough to prove there was a thin white face inside. She had been strewing flowers a trifle too long, I decided; the droop of her lip, the weariness in her rather feline green eyes said it hadn't been all roses, either.

"We're looking for Ted Wood," I said. "Understand you knew him well."

She tried her drink and thought about it, one hand holding back the hair on half a face. "Like well enough to know there wasn't any percentage in it," she conceded finally. "Anyway, he split way back. Good three years ago."

"Where was he going?"

"Back to New York. He said he had family there."

"I'm it," Holly said. "His sister."

Viola wound a long strand of red hair around one finger and regarded her in silence from one eye.

"But he never showed up in New York," Holly added.

"I've heard it's a big place."

"Ted would have contacted me if he'd ever come back.

Besides, he wrote to me from here and said he was going to San Francisco."

"Yeah? Well, so he changed his mind. Anyway, split he did and that's all I know."

I broke in again. "You were shacked up together at the time he left."

"Sure. But no sweat. Like I was as sick of him as he was of me. No offense, honey," she added to Holly. "But he was like one big bushel of nothing."

Holly took it in silence.

"Can you tell us exactly when he left?" I asked.

She parted both sides of hair again so I could see the outraged expression on her face. "You expect me to remember a thing like that?"

"It wasn't a red-letter day in your life, I take it."

"You can say that again!"

"Well, was it summer? July, say? That would have been July, 'sixty-eight."

She picked up a match folder with which Holly must have lit a cigarette while I was gone and began to play with it—tap, tap on the table. "Let's see. . . . Come to think of it, guess it was. Like the middle of summer. Hot. The fan broke and that was the last big fight we had. Over getting the fan fixed." She nodded, very certain now. Fights placed things.

"Ted had come down here from Denver," I said. "Did he ever talk to you about what he had been doing up at Denver?"

"No."

"What time of year did he first show up around here?"

"Well, we were together three, four months. So must have been sometime in early spring."

So far it was checking out, I thought. Dr. Castle had fired him in early spring.

"Did you ever hear from him after he left?"

"You gotta be kidding."

"How was he going to get back to New York? Hitch-hike?"

"What else?"

The next one I slid in as offhandedly as possible. "Did Ted wear china clippers?"

"Huh?"

"You know—false teeth."

"Oh, yeah, sure. Got most of his own knocked out in a fight once." She paused, belatedly wary, and came out of her hair to look at me. "That's a funny question to ask."

"Just a way of checking if he was the same Ted Wood we're looking for. It's not an uncommon name."

She thought about that. "Come to think of it, you never said why you were looking for him, did you?"

"That's simple. Miss Wood here is worried because she hasn't heard from him in a long time. Tell me something else. The bartender said some guy was in here about six weeks ago asking about him. Did he talk to you?"

"No. Nat figured he was fuzz and clammed up." She reached for her glass. "I got a cat waiting for me. I about paid for this drink?"

"Sure. And we're much obliged for the information, Viola."

She sauntered back to the bar and joined her "cat," who'd looked over at us a couple of times while we were talking. He was a big mean-looking blond in boots and a fringed buckskin vest.

"Well," I said to Holly, "you don't want another of these martinis?"

"God, no."

"Then let's split."

I went over to the bar, slid two bills across to Spaniel Eyes. "Give Viola another on me," I said. "Could I get some potato chips?"

The chips rack was at the front of the bar, out of earshot. "Listen," I said, when I had him up there. "Did she talk to that runty guy with shades you mentioned coming in to ask about Ted?"

He nodded. "Yeah, they rapped awhile."

"So never mind telling her I asked," I said. "And keep the change."

Holly was waiting at the door and we walked out to the car.

"You dropped a lot of bread back there," she said, "without getting much—unless it told you more than it told me."

"The bartender said she did talk to Ben Manning. So she lied about that. The rest—well, nothing new, except for the teeth angle, but at least it tallies with what we already know."

I helped her into the car, got in myself and pondered for a moment. "Are you hungry?"

"Not especially."

"Then what say we delay dinner and make a flying trip down to this hippie commune called Cricket Town? You remember? I told you about it this morning."

She nodded. "All right, I'm willing. Do you want to keep up your strength with these potato chips?"

"Might be a good idea. Rattle the bag for us, will you?"

I started the car and we slid off into traffic.

7

BIG ROCK is just off the highway about ten miles south of Astoria. Hardly more than a four-corners settlement, with a gas pump in front of a grocery store. I got directions from the old coot who manned the store. He eyed me disapprovingly.

"You don't look like one of them creeps, mister. What you want up there?"

"It's a business matter."

"Business!" he snorted. "Well, I'm warning you—they're a bad lot. Disgrace to this here whole community."

"Cause you trouble, do they?"

"Well, you believe me I gotta have eyes in the back of my head when they come in here for supplies. Like a bunch of thieving old-time outlaws that's what. Tell you something else." His voice dropped ominously. "They're throwing an orgy up there tonight. I seen half a dozen motorbikes go by in the last hour. Come from all over, they do, when there's an orgy. You best watch your step. I seen you got a lady in the car, too. You just better take care, mister. Ain't no place for decent females."

I assured him I'd take care, and back in the car repeated the conversation to Holly. She laughed.

"Sounds like we picked a good night."

The old coot had been right about one thing: they were coming from all over. A couple of more motorbikes and a jalopy or two whizzed past us as we headed up the dusty gravel road he'd told us to take. We ate dust the rest of the way to the turnoff, where a large wooden arrow was planted in the roadside weeds. It bore no information, but apparently served to direct the initiate.

A narrow dirt road, afflicted with potholes and indetermination, wandering hither and thither to skirt lone trees and boulders, climbed gently from there back through a narrow valley that seemed to be mostly long-unused grazing land. Weeds and sagebrush, rock and dust. Horse-opera country. With the sun long gone over the big ranges, dusk was settling fast.

Abruptly the road leveled out; we went around a last curve of hill, and the lights sprayed the hulk of a big old ranch house up ahead. Bikes and cars were parked helter-skelter in a field of weeds off to the left, and beyond that we could see some ramshackle outbuildings. I wheeled into the parking area.

"Welcome to the orgy," I said.

Lights blazed inside the house and the electronic beat of rock music from stereo speakers hurled itself through the open windows. Hippies, in groups and pairs, were drifting in from the outlying shadows, most of them booted, swathed in ponchos or blankets and carrying lanterns. We got out and straggled along with them toward the long porch of the ranch house. Nobody paid any attention to us. A hirsute loner in cowboy regalia sat on the top step of the porch and gazed at us with supreme indifference when we stopped, letting others pass by and enter the house.

"We're looking for Mr. Baker," I said.

He jerked a thumb over his shoulder. "In there, man."

"That's what I was afraid of," I muttered to Holly, taking her arm firmly.

The steely boom of rock surged at us in a solid wave as we stepped inside. There were probably forty to fifty hippies milling under the colored balls and cylinders hanging from the beamed ceiling of a huge room, others squatting on the floor or leaning against the walls. A fire blazed at one end of the room in a stone hearth big enough to hold a Volkswagen, and at the other end a space had been cleared for a clutter of amps and stereo speakers. A prophet-haired character in a velveteen jacket and striped pants was driving frenetically at a big brown and sunset-blazed guitar and howling to high heaven. Amplified, the noise was enough to knock you down.

I edged along a wall, dragging Holly with me, and mercifully we hadn't gotten too far when the singer collapsed in an excruciating finale. But the shouting and stomping that followed were almost as deafening.

Holly pulled at me and put her face close to my ear. "How do we find him in this crowd?"

"Search me. I'd better ask again. Uh—miss . . ." I tapped a nearby shoulder covered with the waist-length spray of hair that identified it as female. She turned around.

"Grooving, man?" she yelled enthusiastically.

"Yeah, grooving," I yelled back.

She was small and should have been home cheerleading for the high school game. Overloaded with makeup, her eyes were like big exotic flowers in a tiny face.

"I'm looking for Mr. Baker," I said. "A business matter. Could you point him out?"

"You mean Daddy?"

"Oh. You're his daughter?"

She giggled. "Come on, man. He's everybody's daddy. He's the whole world's daddy. Whad ja say you—"

"Can you find him for me?"

"I'll see, if you wanna wait here."

She melted off into the throng. It didn't seem likely she'd ever come back, but we waited. The crowd milled around us like a school of fish in slow motion, a kind of constant pointless back-and-forth shuffling. The air was thick with the reek of pot. We were up near the entertainment end of the room and I could see a pint-size vaquero slinging on a guitar. He adjusted the mike and leaned avidly to his strings. I braced myself for the blast.

Holly squeezed my arm as he compounded his crime by breaking into a hoarse wailing version of "Get Off My Cloud."

"The kid's pretty good," she yelled.

"A lot of voice for his size," I yelled back.

God was not merciful this time; it wasn't until he had finished and the howling and shouting broke out again that Flower-Eyes came oozing out of the crowd. She plucked my arm and indicated we should follow her. We worked our way through the throng to a door at the back of the big room. It led down a long hall. With the door closed you could hear yourself think again, assuming you hadn't suffered permanent brain damage. Flower-Eyes led us to one of several closed doors along the hall, opened it and turned on a light. There was a bed with a couple on it.

"Oops—wrong room," she giggled, rolling the exotic eyes at us slyly. "But don't get uptight, now. Like there's a new morality and all, you know."

"So we've heard," Holly said blandly.

Flower-Eyes turned off the light and closed that door and led us to the next one and switched on the light in there. "This is it. You can wait and Daddy will be along."

It was a very ordinary little office room, except for a few revolutionary posters on the wall. Some filing cabinets and chairs and a large desk. The music sounded decently far off now; thick walls in these old places. We sat.

"Did you get the impression she led us into that bedroom deliberately so she could tell us about the new morality and all?" I asked.

Holly smiled. "Yes, I did. Obviously we were a couple of fuddy-duddies who needed shaking up. It made me feel old."

"Me too. You know the trouble with them is that they swallow their own publicity."

"That's not the only trouble with them," she said dryly. "But honestly, now, if you were sixteen could you pass up that scene out there?"

"Of course not. By the way, how do you feel about the new morality and all?"

She gave me a sidelong look. "Quit fishing, Counselor. Somebody's coming—"

There were heavy steps in the hall, then the door opened and the whole world's daddy walked in. He was corpulent in a solid massive way and it was hard to guess his age— late thirties, maybe. His head was cropped close, but he sported a dark spade beard and heavily tinted saucer-size shades. Costumewise he wasn't among the gaudiest. A sleeveless yellow shirt hugged his barrel chest, and a wide ornate belt tucked in under his corporation held up bell-bottom corduroys.

"I'm Conrad Baker," he said.

I rose and held out a hand. "I'm Phil Kramer, an Astoria attorney, Mr. Baker. This is my client, Miss Wood."

"Happy to know you. I understand you wished to see me on business and I thought we could talk more comfortably back here."

"It was a little noisy," I admitted. "You have quite a place here, Mr. Baker."

"We're not just a hippie commune, Mr. Kramer. Most people don't know that, of course." He went around the desk and seated himself. "You find us on a bash night. But actually we produce here. We are artists and artisans, we work."

"What sort of work?" I asked.

"Weaving, ceramics, candle-making, woodcrafts—we even have a small hand press and dabble in fine bookmaking." He waved a large meaty hand. "There is one difference, of course. We work to live and enjoy the simple life—not to pile up profits."

"That's admirable," I allowed. "And you are the head of this—enterprise?"

"It does take some business skill to function even in a modest way, Mr. Kramer. As, of course, it took some capital to buy up this acreage. But believe me, I don't regret the investment. These kids are happy here, Mr. Kramer. Most of them come from cities where they have been exploited and abused, forced into slum districts, preyed on by greedy landlords and merchants, drug pushers, stupid fuzz. Here they enjoy a measure of protection. I see to that. No hard drugs, no booze, no police persecution. In short, we are living as people were meant to live, Mr. Kramer. Simply, honestly, close to the land, in peace and dignity."

Well pleased with himself, he caressed his beard and smiled. "But I didn't mean to get off on all this. What was it you wished to see me about?"

"We are looking for a man named Ted Wood, Mr. Baker." I launched into a brief rundown, including the description of her brother that Holly had given me, and he listened attentively.

When I had finished my explanations he thought for a minute. Then he shook his head slowly. "I'm sorry, I don't recognize the name, and the description doesn't ring a bell. But I should point out that we've been in operation here only a year, so of course if this man had left the area three years ago it's unlikely I would have run into him." He paused. "Suppose, though, I do a little questioning among my people. They come from all over the country and it's just possible one of them might have encountered this man somewhere."

"Excellent idea," I said. "I'd appreciate it. Here's my card with my phone number." I slid it across to him. "Where did you come from originally, Mr. Baker?"

"Los Angeles—where I dreamed this dream of a commune for almost fifteen years, Mr. Kramer. A sizeable inheritance gave me the opportunity to make it a reality."

"It's a rare man who gets to see his dreams come true. So—congratulations, Mr. Baker."

I rose, and Holly followed suit. He came around the desk and offered his hand again.

"Sorry I couldn't help. But do you know what I wish you'd do—both of you?" He slid his hand out of mine and onto Holly's arm—all very daddylike, of course. "Come see us on a working day. I'd be happy to show you around. We could use some good publicity for a change."

"We might take you up on that," I said, watching his hand administer a little parting squeeze to Holly's arm. "Thanks for seeing us, anyway, Mr. Baker."

"Can you find your way back?"

"Yes, of course."

We went out, closing the door, and started back along the hall. "What big teeth you've got, Daddy," I snarled softly. "And what busy paws."

Holly laughed. "Don't fret, Counselor. This little Red Riding Hood can look out for herself."

A leather-lunged youth in bare feet and torn jeans was belting out "Something's Burning" as we inched our way through the crowd and finally got out onto the porch. The hirsute loner was still there, sitting cross-legged with his back to the wall of the building now.

"Zazen," Holly said.

"What?"

"He's meditating, in the lotus position. It's a Zen thing."

"He'll freeze to death. It's cold out here."

"That's part of it, to test yourself under rigorous conditions. Sink so deeply into thought—or rather into non-thought—that the body has no existence."

"Mine's existing and it's cold," I said. "Come on."

It was good to gulp fresh air again, with stars diamond-bright in a black sky and the frenetic beat of the music fading as we crossed the yard to the parking field. I maneuvered the car out of the jumble of bikes and jalopies and we headed down the dirt road.

"Well, what do you think?" I asked as Holly fired up cigarettes for us.

"I think I'd like to go again and see how they really live. Tents and shacks, I suppose, back in the hills."

I nodded. "But like he said, it's probably better than slum lofts. You wonder what motivates him, though. Does he just enjoy playing God to that bunch of kids?"

"Why not? Everybody secretly wants to be God. He's found a way to do it."

"But why do kids who won't accept establishment authority accept his?"

"Because he isn't asking them to grow up."

"Hm, yes. But what's so wrong with growing up these days?"

"It just doesn't look like any fun."

"It never did."

"Maybe not. But it was the only way to latch onto the goodies—money, power, sex. Now they can have all that without growing up. They can have it with youth and something they think of as freedom thrown in. Can you blame them if they like it that way?"

"No, but I recall what you said about freedom before. That it's a matter of having choices."

"That was me, Counselor—my conception of freedom. There's another, though, that maintains freedom lies in not wanting anything you don't have. These kids go along with that. Cut your wants and you don't even need choices."

"Well," I said, "like it's never simple, heh?"

"Never simple."

I glanced at her. "You've given it a lot of thought. Maybe you should write a book."

"I'm thinking about it." She smiled. "Along with thinking about how hungry I am. Can the next order of business be dinner?"

"It sure can."

We ate at a roadside supper club on the outskirts of

town. The martinis were excellent and the steaks thick and rare.

"It's been a day," Holly said as we lingered over coffee.

"We've covered a lot of ground. You look tired."

"I am. Absolutely bushed."

"Drink up, then, and we'll get back over to the office for your car."

It was close to eleven when we pulled into the lot back of the building. Her rented Mustang was the only car there. I walked her over and tucked her in.

"What's the best way back to my motel?" she asked.

"Turn right when you hit the street and stay on this street until you hit Plover Avenue. Left on Plover will take you straight out there."

"Fine. You'll call me in the morning? My room number is eighteen."

"Will do, but I may be tied up until close to noon, so sleep late."

I waved as she pulled off toward the street, then walked back and got into my own car. I was reaching for the ignition when I saw something I didn't like. A black sedan, moving slowly and without lights, as if it had just pulled out from the curb in front of the building or a little farther back up the street, passed the lot exit and fell in behind Holly's rapidly disappearing lights. Its lights went on as it gathered speed.

Could someone have been following us? Impossible. Certainly there'd been no one behind us coming down from Cricket Town. As for anyone knowing we would be coming back here for her car—that was impossible, too.

Never mind the logic, I thought; when the old sixth sense starts pricking, fall in.

I gunned the motor and shot out into the street.

8

TRAFFIC HERE on Fulton was practically nonexistent this late at night, and the tiny red glow of taillights up ahead were almost certainly those of the black car. I closed the gap gradually and saw that he was keeping a good block behind Holly. She had a heavy foot back of the wheel; we were bowling along well above the speed limit. I knew that I could have been seen coming out of the parking lot, so at Court Street I swung right and over to Amherst. If Holly stayed on Fulton as I'd told her to do it would be easy to pick them up farther on; Amherst parallels Fulton. I gunned it for about six blocks up Amherst, then cut back to Fulton, slowing at the intersection just in time to see the gold Mustang whizz past by. I waited for the other car. Sure enough, black sedan, a man at the wheel. I fell in behind him.

After cutting out as I had done, I doubted he'd have me tagged for a tail. We hit Plover, a main artery where traffic was still fairly brisk. I let a car pass presently, and it stayed between us for twelve blocks or so before turning off. I closed the gap a cautious trifle and made a mental note to give Holly a lecture on her driving. We were doing

at least twenty over the speed limit. Then I saw the High
Tor sign blazing up ahead and she began to slow down for
the turn. The black car ahead of me signaled for left, but
then, to my surprise, picked up speed, veered around her
as she went into the turn, and sped straight on.

Well, even good old sixth sense could lead you up the
creek now and then.

I followed her through the office port anyway, figuring
that as long as I was here I might as well satisfy myself
that she got safely to her room. Parking was double row in
the center of a large courtyard with the two-story buildings
grouped on three sides. She was pulling into an empty space
as I cruised on by and found another space a little farther
up. No sense in scaring her with what had probably been
a flight of imagination on my part. But I cut the motor and
the lights and waited. Her car door slammed shut; she
locked it and came into sight, crossing the lot to the left.
Ornamental lanterns illumined the unit numbers and I
spotted eighteen, a downstairs unit farther up the line. She
went on toward it, swinging along briskly; if she had noticed me following her in, she was certainly paying no attention to me. I watched her fish for the key in the big white
bag and unlock the door. A moment after she'd closed it a
light bloomed palely behind drawn drapes.

I may have been wasting valuable sleeping time, but I
waited another few minutes anyway, on the remote chance
that the black sedan had spotted me for a tail, gone on by
to ditch me, and would be coming back. But it didn't mate-
rialize. Except for the very faint sound of TV somewhere,
the court was quiet, most of the windows dark.

Then abruptly the light went off in unit eighteen. Alarm
prickled along my spine. Nobody fell into bed that fast.

What if somebody had been in there waiting for her—while I watched out here?

Cursing myself for a fool, I shot out of the car and sprinted across the court to the door. I thought it would be locked, but when I grabbed the knob and yanked, it opened. And he was there, the light from the ornamental lantern glinting on the gun in his hand.

"Back up, mister," he snarled.

If I'd had time to think I'd have backed up. I didn't have time to think. I jumped him, clawing for his gun wrist, riding him back into the room. We went down together, me on top, still clutching for his gun wrist with one hand and his face with the other. But he was big and heavy and he heaved me off and scrambled away. I heard Holly scream as I rolled to my feet. In the darkness he was nothing more than a hulking shadow, but I lunged for him anyway, driving my right into his face, catching him on the point of the jaw from the feel of it. It sent him reeling back, but it didn't floor him, and he was flailing at my head with the gun as I swarmed in again, driving at his midriff with both fists. A booted foot came up and caught me in the groin and it was my turn to stagger back. He broke for the door and if I had had any sense I would have let him go, but you don't do your best thinking in the middle of a fight. I lunged after him. He whirled and his uppercut whammed me under the chin, sent me sailing backward onto a chair and over it. He was on me before I could rally, and the gun crashed down on my skull. Light splintered in front of my eyes as I fell and fell—past light, into swimming darkness.

I probably wasn't out for more than a few minutes. When I opened my eyes I was very comfortable in general. That is, flat on my back, with Holly cradling my head in her arms. The lights were on now and the whole room seemed to be spinning slowly and Holly's voice coming from far far away.

"Phil—Phil—for God's sake, Phil, are you all right?"

I mumbled something and raised a hand to the side of my head. Cut and swelling, sticky wet . . .

"You're bleeding," she cried. "Lie still. I'll get a towel."

I wanted to tell her never mind, I liked it this way, a perfumed cleavage pressed close to my face. But my tongue wouldn't move and my thoughts were syrup-slow. She lowered me gently and got up and hurried away into the bathroom. I decided I'd better try to get up and made it onto one elbow and rested, waiting for my head to quit swimming. Finally I hauled myself all the way up and got over to the bed and sat down on the edge. Holly came back with a wet towel.

"Phil, you should lie down—"

"No, I'm all right. Just swab it off a bit. He got away, I suppose."

"Yes." She was swabbing at my head deftly and gently. "Phil, how in the world did you happen to come along?"

I told her. My head was clearing now. I took it out of my hands and looked at her. "My God, Holly!" Ugly red splotches were already darkening into bruises on her throat. "He was choking you."

She touched her neck and winced. "You can say that again. He was hiding in the bathroom and I'd no sooner got the light on than he stepped out and grabbed me, with a hand over my mouth so I couldn't scream. He dragged me over near the door so he could turn out the light. Then he flung me down on the bed and started choking me. I—I thought he was going to kill me, Phil, I really did. He was still choking me when you broke in. Thank God I hadn't locked that door. I never do until I get a light on and make sure everything is all right." She broke off, put both hands to her neck and winced again. "It's sore all the way to my tonsils."

"Did he say anything?" I asked.

"Yes. He said, 'You and that pig get the hell out of town or you'll wish you had.' "

I got to my feet, fairly steady now. "You need doctoring worse than I do," I said grimly. "Sit down here and give me that towel."

I took it into the bathroom, ran water until it was icy cold, soaked the towel and wrung it out quickly. When I came back she had straightened the overturned chair and was sitting in it. She let me wrap the cold towel around her throat and leaned back with a groan.

"It may help the swelling and soreness," I said. "Holly, did you get a look at him?"

"All I really noticed was that he had a kind of scraggly beard. That cap was pulled down on his face." She pointed to where the cap was lying; I'd knocked it off him somewhere along the line. I went over and picked it up, but it was too ordinary to be of the slightest use. I threw it into the wastebasket and did a little prowling, hoping to find something he might have dropped. But no luck. I lit a cigarette and took the desk chair, facing her.

"I can't figure it out. Obviously that car wasn't following you. But somebody was waiting here. He either picked the lock or had a way of getting hold of a key. Yet as far as I can remember we told no one we saw today where you were staying. Right?"

"Right—but wait. Hand me my bag, Phil."

It was lying on the bed, and I brought it to her and she fished carefully in it. "I thought so. While we were at the Lost Cause and you were phoning I lit a cigarette, using a packet of matches I'd picked up in the motel office this morning—High Tor matches. Remember that girl Viola picking up the packet and playing with it? She must have walked off with it, too, because it's not here."

"Viola—sure! She could easily have phoned here, found out your room number and sent some hippie goon—maybe even that bird she was with. Remember him? He was big and blond and wore boots."

"But I don't think he was bearded."

"Well, we'd never get a line on him anyway, so I don't suppose it matters who he was. The thing is, Viola sent him. Another thing that fits. What was it he said to you? 'You and that pig get out of town.' The Lost Cause was the only place we visited where I didn't identify myself as an attorney. So she figured I was fuzz—like Ben Manning." I broke off. "How does your throat feel?"

"Kind of numb now—from the cold."

"You can't ask for better than that. I'll fix another towel."

"All right, but then you've got to go, Phil. You took some lumps, too, and we both need rest."

My adrenalin soared again when I changed the cold pack. The bastard had really gouged her. Hopped-up, probably—and how far he might have gone if I hadn't broken in didn't bear thinking about.

"I hope I get my hands on him again," I muttered. "I just hope to God I do."

She looked at me and there was a shadow of fear in her eyes. "I think I'm getting you into something pretty messy, Phil. I hadn't realized that anything like this could happen. It proves somebody doesn't like what we're doing."

"I think it also proves we're onto something. You wouldn't want to quit now?"

"No—not if you're still game."

I leaned over and kissed her on the forehead. "I'm still game. Now let me out, put the chain on and don't open that door for anything, you understand?" I paused. "Of course, if you're afraid to be alone here I could be persuaded to stay."

She smiled ruefully. "Of two perils you could easily prove the worse. Go home, Counselor."

By the time I got across town to my apartment my head was hammering again and my left leg was stiffening at the knee. I hauled myself to the bathroom mirror. A budding lump and bruise over the left eye, too. I swallowed some aspirin and limped to the kitchen. There was a note on the table from my faithful cleaning lady, Mrs. Mabie.

> Brung you some of my cinnamon rolls. In the bread box. Don't forget.
>
> Yours, Mrs. M.
>
> P.S. I glued up that busted cup you threw in the junk. Leave it sit for 24 hours. *Waste not, want not.*

I poured a double Scotch and wrapped some ice cubes in a towel. Nursing the lump with the cold pad, I sprawled on my sofa, sipped the drink and fell to thinking. By the time I'd finished the Scotch the ice was melting and water dripping down my face.

I gave up the thinking and went to bed.

9

THE ALARM exploded at seven and I piled out. My knee would take a little limbering up and I still had a dull headache, but it could have been worse. I swallowed aspirin again and put on some coffee. By the time I'd showered and shaved it was ready, strong and hot, and I sat down to it with Mrs. Mabie's beautiful cinnamon rolls. I had the cup on its way to my lips the third time when it broke, and I realized I'd thoughtlessly used the one Mrs. Mabie had "glued up." I mopped the table and threw the cup remains back in the junk. *Glue not, rue not*.

Mickey was watering the begonia on her desk when I got to the office.

"What happened to you?"

"Oh . . ." The bump and bruise over my eye had looked better this morning, but it did show. "Ran into a door, what else? Lee here?"

"Not yet."

"How were things yesterday?"

"Rough," she sighed. "He didn't break down. How long can it last?"

"It's never lasted more than three days, so cheer up. This is the second, one to go."

"You're supposed to call Hathaway and Hathaway—something about some Emerson securities."

"Will do."

"And Mr. Carmady and his partner are coming at ten-thirty. I've got the contract ready."

"Good."

I went on into my own cubicle, hung up my jacket and went to the files for the Emerson folders. I'd barely sat down and opened them when Mickey tapped and came in.

"Mrs. Rodney Emerson called and wants an appointment. I said you weren't here yet and I'd phone back. She sounded pretty darned upset."

"I believe it," I groaned. "She's the one I'm betting will smuggle Rough-on-Rats into Nightingale's tuna fish. Well, call her back, say I can't possibly see her until Friday. That'll give her time to cool down."

"Right," Mickey said, but lingered on, looking meditative. "You know, I just had a thought, Phil."

"Don't panic," I said gently. "It will probably go away."

"No, I'm serious. As I understand it, old Mrs. Emerson tied up one hundred thousand dollars to maintain the house and help to take care of Nightingale in her—uh—familiar surroundings as long as she lives."

"Correct."

"Suppose Nightingale should have kittens."

"Ye gods. She's too old. Besides, she's probably been spayed."

"Six years isn't too old. And do you *know* that she's been spayed?"

"Well, no. But I do know she's never let out to mingle with the riffraff."

"Nevertheless, just suppose."

"Suppose what?"

"Suppose she *does* have kittens. Would they inherit Nightingale's—uh—legacy, if Nightingale should pass on? If they did, all that money could be tied up for another twenty years, couldn't it?"

"Listen," I said darkly. "Do you want me to cut my throat? If the answer is no, then just kindly leave. Like disappear—go away and try not to do any more thinking."

Mickey shrugged. "Okay, but I think you should give some thought to the legal aspects of this."

She was at the door before I called, "Wait a minute—"

"Yes?"

"Just for the sake of your own peace of mind," I said nonchalantly, "why don't you phone the house and ask Mrs. Highland, the housekeeper, if Nightingale has been spayed? I mean, just so you won't be worrying over anything so ridiculous."

"Right," Mickey said, and went away.

I phoned Hathaway and Hathaway, got into a long tangle of facts and figures, hung up finally and stared at the sheet of notes in front of me. Somehow I just wasn't in the mood for other people's money. I closed the folder and got up and put on my jacket and stalked out to where Mickey was now busy at the typewriter.

"I have to go see someone. I'll be back in time for Carmady. Did you phone Mrs. Highland?"

"Yes, and Nightingale has never been spayed. Old lady Emerson didn't believe in it. But she assured me Nightingale is never allowed out, so I guess we needn't worry."

And one worry less, I decided, as I descended the stairs to the parking lot, wasn't to be sneezed at.

It takes more than peanuts to be balmy at the Four Pines. Sitting high on a wooded hill out on Pennock Road, it has the air of a private estate, with an elegant drive sweeping up the hill to a château-like main building which was, in fact, once the home of a now long-deceased local tycoon. Back of this, discreet little footpaths lead away to small cottages half hidden among the trees. An orderly mopping the deserted entrance lobby of the big building directed me to the office of a Mrs. Buffington, where I introduced myself and said I wished to see Mr. Rufus Langley. Having impressed it on me that this was not a proper visiting hour, she decided to make an exception to their very strict ruling about visiting hours, did some phoning, and took me back to the orderly still mopping in the lobby.

"Clarence, show this gentleman over to Miss Sands in three, will you?"

"Yes, ma'am, I'll just get my helmet."

"Dear God," the lady said, rolling her eyes. Then she added to me, "When the patients are able we let them help with the work."

"I see."

Clarence had gone back to a table for his helmet, which was a bright-orange hard-hat. He put it on and we went out and started up one of the footpaths.

"Why the helmet?" I asked.

"Birds."

"Birds?"

"Think about it. There are millions of them flying around up there, aren't there? And they've all got to die sometime."

"Well, yes."

"So what happens? They die and they fall. You think I want to get beaned by one of them?"

"I guess I never thought about it," I muttered.

We reached one of the cottages. "This is it," he said. "You don't happen to have a cigarette?"

"Sure." I proffered my pack and he took two and carefully stashed them in the pocket of his white jacket.

"There's another thing," he said.

"What's that?"

"Every time you swallow a mouthful of food you could choke to death. It's a miracle if you don't."

"I guess I can't deny it," I admitted. "Just never thought about that either."

"That's the whole trouble. Nobody really thinks. But I do, I think all the time. I could tell you a lot of things I'll bet you never thought about."

"I'm in a hurry right now," I said. "Maybe some other time."

"Suit yourself." He gestured toward the cottage. "Just ring the bell there. So long."

He trotted off down the path with his orange helmet. I'd felt better before I met him.

A brisk bosomy party unlocked and opened the door when I rang. "You're the Mr. Kramer to see Mr. Langley?"

"Yes, ma'am."

She locked the door as soon as I was in. "This way." She led me down a hall to one of several doors, paused with her hand on the knob. "You understand about Mr. Langley? Harmless, but often confused."

"Oh, yes—yes, I know."

"Don't stay too long, please. They sometimes get overexcited." She opened the door and called out in a loud cheerful voice, "Mr. Kramer to see you, Mr. Langley. Isn't that nice?"

It was a large comfortable bedroom–sitting room. A man sat clacking busily at a typewriter on a desk by the windows. He stopped and peered at us over the top of large black-rimmed spectacles.

"A visitor for you, Mr. Langley," the nurse boomed cheerfully again. "A Mr. Kramer."

"Ah, yes, of course." He rose quickly, a tall thin man, slightly stooped. "Mr. Kramer, yes." It was as if he had been expecting me.

"Have a nice visit," the nurse yelled jovially and went out, closing the door.

Rufus Langley slid the spectacles up on his forehead and beamed at me. "So! I wondered how long it was going to take you."

"Take me?"

He winked slyly. "You know. To catch on."

"Catch on?" I was beginning to wonder who was balmy.

"Well, you got my messages, didn't you? You know—the poems. 'Here's the castle, look inside . . .' "

"Oh—the poems. Let's see, now. You wrote those poems?"

"Of course I wrote them. I am a writer, you're probably aware of that. See here." He went to the desk and tapped a fat pile of papers. "This is the sequel I'm working on now."

"The sequel?"

"To my first book—*Gone with the Wind*."

"I see. You wrote that?"

"Good heavens, yes. Oh, I realize it's not generally known. But you see, back in 'thirty-eight when I had finished the book I sent the manuscript to this cousin of mine in Atlanta to read. He lost it on a bus and it was never recovered. We know now what happened, though. The Mitchell woman found it and proceeded to publish it as her own. Oh, I'm not blaming her," he added generously. "Especially as she finally admitted the truth, though *that* never got into the papers, you may be sure." He waved airily. "But we have other things to talk about. Here—sit down, Mr. Kramer."

There were two comfortable lounge chairs; he had pulled one around for me so they were facing, and he perched himself on the edge of the other, which brought us practically knee to knee. "Now tell me," he began briskly. "What did you think of my little plan? About the poems, I mean."

"Well, I was—uh—somewhat puzzled. That is, until I caught on, of course."

He nodded happily. "I understand. But it seemed the only way left. No one here would listen to me. And I couldn't just let her get away with it, could I? I'd heard about you, Mr. Kramer, that is, I'd read about you in the paper, and I figured you were just the kind of clever young man who could help me." He leaned closer. "First of all, I've got a little cash tucked away. Insurance money I collected when I had an auto accident. I'm willing to spend every cent of it to get that woman put behind bars."

"What woman?"

It dashed him ever so slightly that I'd had to ask, but he rallied quickly. "Why, Mavis Castle, of course. You realize she killed my brother—my half brother, I should say— Dr. David Castle. But perhaps I should tell you the whole story."

"I'm acquainted with the case, Mr. Langley. In fact, I've been doing a little probing into it myself."

"You have?" He beamed at me again; I was back on the

clever-young-man list. "Oh, that's excellent. Then, with what I can tell you, Mr. Kramer, that woman is going to get her comeuppance at last." He broke off and looked at me sternly. "Not that she's the only one. There's a man involved, too. Her lover. They planned it together, no question of that."

"You mean Leslie Rainier."

"So you know about him!"

"Yes. But it seems there is one little problem, Mr. Langley, regarding this theory of yours. They both had alibis for the Saturday night on which the fire occurred."

He held up a large pale hand. "Wait, now—wait. Just because that fire wasn't discovered until next morning doesn't mean it was started late Saturday night like the authorities claimed."

"Well, experts on these matters generally know what they're talking about, Mr. Langley."

"Oh, bosh. They found some smoldering ruins. They couldn't possibly have told exactly how long they had been smoldering or exactly when that fire was started. Do you know why they assume it started after dark? Simply because nobody in the vicinity had noticed the smoke by daylight. What does that prove? Nothing—except that the few people in that vicinity who might have happened to see it didn't happen to see it."

There was at least a grain of truth in that, so I said nothing. He reached over and tapped my knee.

"That fire started in the afternoon, Mr. Kramer—while Mavis was up there. Take my word for it. I *know*."

"As I understand it, Mr. Langley, neither Mavis nor anyone else went up there at any time over the weekend."

I was messing up the script so badly that he had to pull the spectacles down from his forehead and reevaluate me through the lenses. Judging by his frown, it was nip and tuck for a minute. Then his expression relaxed. He smiled, very confidently and knowingly. "Bosh again, Mr. Kramer —utter bosh. You see, I can prove Mavis went up there Saturday afternoon."

"How?"

"By the typewriter. The one David had taken to have repaired."

"I don't think I understand."

"Well, it was like this. David had been here to see me a week before he died. My typewriter had broken down and he took it back to Denver with him to get it fixed. I couldn't do a thing here without it and I was pretty impatient. So Friday morning I asked the nurse to phone him at his office and ask about it. He told her to tell me he couldn't get it from the repair shop until Saturday afternoon."

"I see. Well?"

"But they found the typewriter in the debris of the fire."

"*That* typewriter?"

"Of course. I made sure when they took me up to David's funeral. His own portable was in his study, right on the desk, and Mavis' was in her bedroom. I asked her—without letting on, you know, why I wanted to know."

"Then I take it you didn't—uh—discuss this matter with Mavis, didn't make an accusation or anything of that sort?"

He straightened in the chair and looked at me bitterly. "What good would it have done? She'd have lied her way out of it."

"Well, let's suppose it was your typewriter. Maybe after you called David's office that morning he phoned and got the repairman to hurry up with the job so he was able to pick it up at noon before he left."

He shook his head slowly and earnestly. "Mr. Kramer, if David had gotten the typewriter Friday morning he would have rushed right down to me before he ever went to the cabin. He *knew* how anxious I was to get it."

"Didn't you have another machine to use while that one was gone?"

"Oh, Dr. Alexander had offered me one, but I refused. I couldn't have worked with anything but my own machine. It's personal between a writer and his typewriter, Mr. Kramer—very, very personal."

I thought a minute. It would be easy to discard the whole story as a figment of his imagination. I doubted it was that. More likely seeds of fact, watered with some confusion. The problem was to sort the seeds out from the confusion. "Let's see if I have this straight now, Mr. Langley," I said finally. "You think Mavis got the typewriter from the repair shop on Saturday afternoon and took it up to the cabin, at which time she—uh—set the fire to kill her husband."

"Exactly."

"But why would Mavis have taken it up there? Why not have brought it down here to you?"

He recoiled. "Mavis come here! I should say not. We weren't on those kind of terms, Mr. Kramer. You see, I never trusted her. She was the wrong woman for David, and I saw that right from the start. As for her, she hated me and did her best to turn David against me. She would never have come here, I can assure you of that."

"If things were that bad between you and Mavis it seems a little odd she would have bothered to pick up the type-writer and drag it all the way up to the cabin."

"Oh, David must have made her do it, you can be sure of that. And of course he would have brought it straight

down to me Saturday night, undoubtedly that was what he
was planning to do. But he never had the chance. Because
she set that fire while she was up there."

Given Rufus Langley's frame of reference, the logic was
unassailable. By any other frame of reference it had more
holes than a peek-a-boo blouse. Intent on a weekend drunk,
Dr. Castle wouldn't have been that concerned about getting
a typewriter back to his balmy brother. Chances were he'd
picked the machine up earlier in the week and had only been
stalling when he'd told the Four Pines nurse it wouldn't be
ready until Saturday.

Pointing out any of this to Rufus Langley would be a
waste of time, of course. So I nodded sagely. "I see. Did you
speak to anyone else of all this?"

"Oh, yes, I told Dr. Alexander. As usual, he thought I
was just mixed up about things. And he got me another
typewriter and told me to forget about it." He pursed his
lips mournfully. "I knew my own machine was gone beyond
recall, so I had to do the best I could with this one, but it
hasn't been easy. Anyway, you can see the fix I was in, Mr.
Kramer. I had to find somebody who would listen to me. So
now you think about it. You're a smart young man. You
just think about it."

"I certainly will, Mr. Langley. One thing that still puzzles
me, though. Why would Mavis have wanted to do such a
terrible thing?"

"To get the money. There was all that insurance, double
indemnity for accidental death. She was a greedy woman.
And with that lover of hers to egg her on . . . Besides, David
told me something in strict confidence the last time he was
here." He motioned me forward and leaned forward himself,
dropping his voice to a stage whisper. "He said he was going

to divorce her." Having produced that, he leaned back and looked at me triumphantly. "So you see, don't you? She was desperate—she and that Rainier."

"The way I hear it, Mr. Langley," I ventured, "Dr. Castle wasn't a model of marital fidelity himself."

He waved that away with a large generous flap of his hand. "We're men of the world, aren't we, Mr. Kramer?"

"You mean what was permissible for Dr. Castle wouldn't be permissible for Mrs. Castle."

"Of course."

"But a court of law might have viewed it differently, Mr. Langley. In which case, Mavis might very well have gotten a good financial settlement. That is, if Dr. Castle was well off. I'm wondering about that too. I realize he was a successful physician, but I suppose they may have lived pretty extravagantly."

"She had him in debt most of the time, Mr. Kramer. You may take my word for that. As fast as David made it, she spent it. So of course there were financial difficulties. Why, at one time David even talked to me about the possibility of moving me to a less expensive place. Believe you me, I blew my top about that. I said—"

"Oh, David was footing the bill here?" I interrupted.

"Of course, though let me make it plain it was family money he was using, so I was perfectly entitled to—"

"Who's footing the bill now?" I asked.

"David's will left a provision for it. You just bet she would have broken that if she could have, but she couldn't."

"Did she try?"

"No, but only because she knew she couldn't."

I sighed. Portraits in solid black are never very convincing. I wondered if it would be worth trying to get his reaction on my insurance-fraud theory, and decided it wouldn't be. He had it figured out the way he liked it and it wasn't likely that he would even consider another version. In any case, the nurse rapped on the door at that point and then opened it and put her head in.

"Almost time for your therapy, Mr. Langley," she yelled. "Had a good visit?"

I rose. "Guess it's time I leave, Mr. Langley. But I'll certainly think about all this."

"And you'll let me know what you find out?" he asked eagerly.

"Of course. You take care of yourself meanwhile. And good luck with the book."

The nurse accompanied me down the hall to unlock the door. "It was nice of you to come," she said. Ordinary-volume level now; the shouting was for the patients, don't ask me why. "He doesn't have visitors too often."

"No family at all, I suppose, since his brother died."

"Oh, Mrs. Castle, that's his sister-in-law, comes occasionally."

So much for that. I walked down the path to where I'd left the car in front of the main building. You might be able to sort truth from delusion. With businesslike lies thrown in to bolster his story you didn't have much of a chance. He had a big down on Mavis Castle, and everything he'd told me could have been fabricated around that one fact.

"Hey!" It was Clarence. He was sweeping a walk that went around the side of the building, still in his orange helmet, of course. I had the feeling he'd been waiting for me.

He walked over. "Another thing I wanted to mention."

"What's that?"

"Gravity. We figure it's going to last, don't we? Just because it's always been around. But what if it gives out one of these days and up we go—you, me, everybody—like a bunch of balloons? And where does all *that* end?"

"Clarence," I said, "you worry too much."

"Somebody has to."

"So if we're up there with the birds no bird is going to fall and bean us. That's some consolation, isn't it?"

He leaned on the broom and pondered. "I'd have to think that out. You don't happen to have a cigarette?"

I let him pluck two more from my pack and noticed as he stored them away that the first two were still intact.

"When do you get to smoke them?" I asked.

"*Smoke* them! I wouldn't smoke one of these for anything. They're killers."

"Then why did you ask for them?"

"I'm trying to help you. The ones you gave me you won't smoke. Right? And it could be the difference between life and death. Right?"

"Well, there's certainly something to it," I conceded.

"The thing is, you've got to *think*," he said.

"Right!" I said, and climbed into the Merc and headed down the drive.

You had to say one thing for a visit to a place like this. It gave you a whole new slant on a lot of things.

10

I HAD TWENTY minutes before Carmady was due when I got back to the office. I phoned Holly. She was just up, had yet to shower, dress and eat.

"No more visitors?"

"No, nothing, thank God. But you should see my neck this morning. It's a sight to behold. I'll have to wear something that will keep it covered. Are you all right?"

"I'm fine. Suppose I pick you up there in about an hour and a half?"

"I'll be ready."

I hung up and went into Lee's cubicle. The air was pure and clean. He was hunched over a drift of papers on his desk, writing. Neither pipe nor ashtray was in evidence. Obviously he'd survived the night.

"How's it going?" I asked.

He continued to write. "How's *what* going?"

I know when I'm being challenged to knock a chip off his shoulder, so I tactfully declined, pulled a chair around instead.

"About her of the thousand-dollar retainer," I began.

He dropped the pencil and swung around in his chair. "Yes. I gather you're off on one of your diversions."

"I'd hardly call it that. The lady had a problem. I've done a little probing and it's gotten interesting. Ties in with those Mad Poet letters. You see . . ."

I told it like it was. I could see I wasn't convincing him that I wasn't off on a diversion.

"You know, don't you," he observed acidly when I had more or less concluded my story, "that insurance investigators out to save the company five hundred thousand wouldn't leave a stone unturned?"

"Yes, but you have to look at it this way, too. You can turn a stone over one year and it's clean as a whistle underneath. Turn it over a few years later and it can be crawling with many interesting things. Remember the Dalloway case. His car went off a cliff up around Central City. They found him well roasted in it and the widow duly collected the insurance. Five years later somebody spotted him walking down a street in Buffalo, New York. With a lady friend of former days, now his wife, of course. He'd gotten careless and come back from Canada. That's what always happens. Somebody eventually gets careless."

"That was slightly different. He'd used a dead-and-buried body. He wanted his wife and kids to have the insurance money. This is something else again—the two of them plotting to share the money."

"I'm not sure it's that. I've got an open mind on whether she's his accomplice or his victim. All I'd swear to at this point is that somebody is siphoning money off her."

He picked up the pencil and began stabbing at the desk with it. "If I were going to waste my time on it, which needless to say I wouldn't be going to do, I'd check out former lady friends."

"Excellent idea," I said heartily. "I knew you'd come up with something useful."

"Spare me the soft soap. As for this Manning. You've found his body, of course. You do know he's dead—and murdered."

"Not quite, no. That's merely an educated guess at this point. But give me time. I've been on it less than twenty-four hours."

"Which reminds me. Perhaps you could give me a rough estimate of just how long you figure you're going to be occupied with this little diversion. Not that I like to spoil your fun and games. But we *are* running a law firm here."

I paddled air. "Who knows? Depends on what the lady wants to spend. As long as she's spending, why should we worry?"

"Carmady's due in a few minutes."

"I'm taking care of it."

"And Erskine this afternoon."

"I thought you might take that. I have to run up to Denver around noon. Unless you think I can do more for the firm by busying myself with Erskine's tax-evasion mess."

He swung around to the papers on his desk. "Proceed with caution," he barked.

Holly Wood was ready and waiting by the time I got over to the High Tor. She was wearing a white turtleneck sweater to hide the bruises, plus a swirled mini-skirt and knee-high white boots. The big white bag was slung over one shoulder; love beads and a huge bone-colored bracelet that practically covered her forearm completed the ensemble.

"If I may comment on your appearance with a simple old-fashioned exclamation," I said, "wow!"

"Thank you," she said. "What are we up to today?"

"I've already been at work, though it probably wasn't worth the trouble," I said, and told her about my visit to Rufus Langley. "I don't see any way to check it out except to go to Mrs. Castle, who would almost certainly assure us she did not go up there with Rufus' typewriter. So suppose we try something else—namely, get a line on some of the doctor's lady friends. Especially the last one. The one who, if I'm on the right track with insurance fraud, just might know something about it. Or, even more interestingly, just might have vanished into the blue yonder with him."

"And how do we go about this?"

"Well, I expect his widow would be the wrong one to approach. But office nurses, like private secretaries, generally have an inside track on what's what with the boss's love life. So I think we'll try the starchy Miss Parker again."

"You think *she* might have had a fling with him herself? Doctors and nurses, you know."

"I hadn't thought of that, but I wouldn't say it's impossible. She's not young, but she's not a bad-looking woman, either—if a man had a way past the starch. Tell you what we'll do. We'll zero in with tact and dignity and see what happens."

We were in Denver by one and went straight to the Medical Arts Building, only to learn from an elderly biddy now at the desk that Irene Parker was home with a cold. Keeping an askance eye on Holly's costume, she informed us that she was not free to dispense Miss Parker's home address.

"I suppose it's in the phone book," I said.

"Oh, yes."

"Well, just to save me looking couldn't you tell me what it is?"

"Rules are rules," she said primly.

So we descended to the lobby phone booth and learned that Miss Parker lived out on North Garden.

"Willing to risk a cold in the interests of truth?" I asked Holly.

"Why not? Couldn't be a better time to have a flannel rag around my throat. Are you willing to risk me with a red nose?"

"I think," I said, "you might be sort of cute even with that."

We headed over to North Garden. The place proved to be a large square stucco house on a dignified tree-lined street. It set well back on an imposing lot and we rolled up a driveway past a tall hedge to a porte cochere laden with vines. There was a double garage, doors closed, up at the end of the driveway, back of the house. Everything looked substantial and well kept. We stopped under the porte, got out and stood on the one little step to ring the side doorbell. After a moment Irene Parker appeared.

"Whad is this?" she demanded. She was clutching a chenille robe around her and sounded not only nasal but annoyed.

"You remember us, Miss Parker?"

"Yes, bud whad do you wand?"

"We'd like to talk to you again, Miss Parker. I know it's an imposition when you aren't feeling well, but we're pressed for time and it *is* important."

She agreed that it was an imposition. Nevertheless, she

unlatched the screen door and let us into a square reception hall.

"I'be just gedding myself some dea and doast in the living room. If you don'd mind."

I assured her we didn't mind and she took us into the living room, where indeed her tea and toast stood on a tray on a card table in front of an old-fashioned brick fireplace. Some kindling was snapping away on the grate.

"I'be been feeling chilled," she said. "Sid down, if you please. And eggscuse be for one bobent."

She went away and we heard some distant honking and I sincerely hoped it was clearing clogged passages. I also noted, as she returned, that even out of uniform and with a severe cold she managed to look starched and authoritative —perhaps because she carried her tall heavyset body so erectly. Might Dr. Castle, I was wondering, have found her attractive enough for a fling, as Holly had suggested? I decided he might have.

"Do go ahead with your lunch, Miss Parker," I said.

"I'll just drink some tea. I find I'm not hungry after all." For the moment clogged passages were improved. She took the already filled cup and sat down in a chair with it, facing us. "Well? What is it you want?"

"I'm going to ask you a very frank question, Miss Parker. Were you entirely satisfied that Dr. Castle's death was an accident?"

It didn't rattle her in the least. "Of course. It was thoroughly investigated."

"There was a great deal of insurance money involved," I said.

She took a sip of tea. "Well—what of it?"

"Dr. Castle's wife, I understand, was interested in another

man. And the doctor himself, we have heard, had been involved with other ladies. Correct?"

I waited for her face to register something. I might as well have waited for a lamppost to lean down and pat my head. She only nodded. "These things always seem to get around, don't they?" Then she put the cup down on a table and leaned back. There was a faint gleam of curiosity in her eyes. "Do I take it you feel unsatisfied that Dr. Castle's death was what it appeared to be?"

"I'm beginning to wonder, Miss Parker."

"You think it might have been foul play?"

"That, or an insurance swindle. Suppose the body of this man we can't find, this Ted Wood, was used in that fire and Dr. Castle is alive somewhere."

That did get a reaction. "Oh—nonsense," she said sharply. "A man like Dr. Castle, with a successful career— why, that's simply ridiculous."

"He was a heavy drinker," I said. "And it does seem to have been hurting his practice. You'd know about that, Miss Parker."

"It's not anything I could discuss," she said firmly.

"Well, think about it. And then throw in marital troubles and very likely some financial troubles." I paused. "Wouldn't you say that it's at least possible Dr. Castle might have wanted to slip away into a whole new life and a whole new person? With the insurance money to finance it, of course."

She wasn't stupid. She sat and thought about it for a minute, finally nodded. "Oh, I suppose it's remotely possible. But that would mean—" She stopped.

"Mean what, Miss Parker?" I asked.

"He couldn't have done it without Mrs. Castle's cooperation."

I nodded. "It is reasonable to assume she helped. He pulled the dirty work, she promised him a share of the insurance money. But it could also have happened the other way. He did it without her knowledge, and after she received the insurance money he let her know what he had pulled and demanded a share of the money. She'd have had to play ball, knowing that if she exposed him nobody in the world would believe she hadn't been a party to the fraud."

Her eyes, which could have been pretty if they hadn't chosen to employ the cold hard stare, were fixed on me. "You have talked to Mrs. Castle about all this?"

"Yes, to both her and the man she was involved with, still seems to be involved with—Leslie Rainier. They denied it vigorously, of course. Yet I was struck by the fact that Mrs. Castle seems to be living very modestly for someone who only lately collected five hundred thousand in insurance. I was also struck by the fact that she has never married this man Rainier."

Miss Parker's face contorted. She grabbed a handkerchief from the robe pocket in time to smother a series of mighty sneezes. After which she blew delicately—and not with complete success.

"Well," she observed finally, "if you are right about all this, Dr. Castle cerdainly seems to have godden away with id, doesn't he?" She paused. "I don't subbose there's a way in the world you could ever prove id."

"Not unless we could track Dr. Castle down somehow. Which brings me to another point. If we could locate the lady with whom Dr. Castle was involved at the time he died, or supposedly died, she might be able to tell us something. That is, if he didn't take her along."

"Dake her along?" Irene Parker gave a short humorless laugh. "An inderesting idea. Bud you can forged id. He wouldn't have valued any woban enough to dake her along. He was constitutionally incapable of love or fidelity."

I stuck my neck out. "You appear to know whereof you speak, Miss Parker?"

"You bed I know," she said grimly. Then, with a shrug of her heavy shoulders, she added flatly, "All righd. I had an affair with him once. Does that surbrise you? Probably it does. I'm nod cude and fluffy. I'm nod even young. But I *was* around. That was enough for a man like David. Whoever was handy—" She broke it off. "But led me assure you of one thing. I wasn't the lady in his life at the dime he died. Our affair had been over long ago."

"Who was the lady in his life at that time, Miss Parker?"

"Her name was Virginia Logan. Thad came out at the dime of the invesdigation. She had been working as a private secretary in the office of a real-estate firm. Bud she had left down several months before Dr. Castle died."

"Where had she gone?"

"Back to Michigan—some small down where her family lived. Her mother had cancer, I understand, and she was going back to dake care of her." She paused. "So the story wend. And I subbose the invesdigators checked it oud."

"Do you remember the name of the town?" I asked.

She thought a minute. "Arlington, I think. But she's probably gone from there long ago."

"She never came back here to this area?"

"Nod to my knowledge. But then I did nod know her."

"One other thing, Miss Parker," I said. "I talked to Rufus Langley, Dr. Castle's half brother. He had quite a story about a typewriter of his that he claims was destroyed in the fire."

I related it to her. She listened rather blankly. Then she shrugged.

"I can'd honestly say I know anything aboud the matter. Bud I would guess David had picked up the typewriter earlier in the week and didn'd wand him to know it, because Rufus would have eggsbected him to rush righd down there with id. He could be a derrible nuisance, you know."

"In other words, when the nurse called from the Four Pines Dr. Castle just stalled and said he couldn't get it until Saturday."

"Yes, I'd say that's very likely. I'd seen David stall him off thad way on other occasions when Rufus was pestering him aboud something."

"Even assuming, though, that Dr. Castle had the machine in his car, why would he have taken it into the cabin?"

"Oh, well, you see he often brebared babers for medical conferences and such. He sobetimes worked on these up at the cabin."

"Did he keep a typewriter up there?"

"I doubt that; the place was occasionally broken indo and vandalized. It didn'd pay to keeb things of value there. I subbose he would have daken his home pordable along when he indended to work. Perhabs that last dime he may have decided to do sobe wriding after he god up there and remembered he had Rufus's machine in the car."

I nodded; it was about the way I'd figured it anyway. She groped for her handkerchief again, blew less delicately this time and with improved results.

"You might remember one thing," she said. "Rufus Langley disliked Mrs. Castle intensely."

"I gathered that," I said. "By the way, both Mrs. Castle and Leslie Rainier seem to have alibis for the night of the fire. I suppose you do, too, Miss Parker."

"Oh, naturally," she said dryly. "As a matter of fact, my father was still living at that time. He had been an invalid for years, given to sleeping all day while I was at work, and giving me a rough time at night when I badly needed my sleep. Believe me, there wasn't the slightest chance of me getting out of here nights," she concluded grimly. Then she looked at Holly. "I take it from all this that you haven't found any trace of your brother?"

"None, Miss Parker."

"But he *was* a drifter—"

"Yes, but he had always kept in some touch with me through the years. It's not like him to have suddenly changed on that."

"Incidentally, too," I said, "we learned from Mrs. Castle that Dr. Castle later found that money he'd accused Ted Wood of stealing. He told Mrs. Castle he wanted to find Ted and make reparation, and it is just possible he did. Which means he may have known where Ted was, and when—and if—he dreamed up this swindle, well, he might have felt Ted would serve a nice purpose. Probably so far as he knew Ted had no family or close ties and wouldn't be missed if he disappeared."

She was silent for a moment. "Well, I still think it's all utter nonsense, but . . . who knows?" She shrugged, then passed a hand rather wearily over her forehead.

"We've tired you and I'm sorry," I said, rising. Holly followed suit. "If I might bother you with one more question, could you tell me how to get up to the Castle cabin?"

"Not exactly. But I know it's near a small town called Piñon Point, and I expect you could inquire there. Of course, I'm not sure Mrs. Castle still owns the property, but you could probably find out about that too."

She took us to the door. "You can turn around in that space by the garage," she said.

"Thank you and goodbye, Miss Parker. I hope you'll be feeling better soon."

We got into the car, turned around and slid back down the driveway.

"You can't say she tried to conceal the fact she'd had an affair with Dr. Castle," Holly observed.

"No, but she knew that we could easily find it out, so let's not give her too much credit."

"I wonder about her, Phil. Suppose even though their affair was long over, as she put it, she was still carrying a torch. Or doing a long slow burn because he threw her over for somebody else."

"And so one night she finally went up and burned the place down around him?"

"Well, it's a thought, isn't it? A good stiff pill could have settled Daddy for the night, so that's not much of an alibi."

"Yes, only it washes my insurance swindle down the drain. And there are a lot of things that substantiate that theory, Holly."

She turned her head away with a sigh. "I know. I guess I'm just looking for something that would give me a chance to believe Ted is still alive. Well—what now?"

"A check on this Virginia Logan, first of all. She left town a few months before Dr. Castle died, and despite la Parker's certainty that the doctor would not have taken anyone along into his new life I'm not that sure. I want to know what became of Virginia Logan and I propose to find out."

"How?"

"The fuzz have their uses. Let's find a phone booth."

11

I FOUND one over on Federal and dialed Homicide down at Astoria. Jerry Howe, just back from lunch, was in a fairly mellow mood for him.

"How were things at Cricket Town, Counselor?"

"Groovy, man. We hit a rock party. You should have been there. Lotsa grass and chicks. Will you make a check on something for me?"

"Sure, if it isn't too idiotic."

"It's very important. In the late spring of 1968 a woman named Virginia Logan left Denver to go back to her home town, Arlington, Michigan, and take care of her sick mother. I want to know exactly what became of Virginia Logan, and the easiest way should be you making a nice phone call to the chief of police at Arlington who out of professional courtesy will delve into the matter."

"I need a reason."

"Surprise me and think one up yourself."

"Counselor, what the hell *are* you up to?"

"I'm doing a trace job on a guy who has been missing for three years."

"Who?"

"Tut, tut—you know I can't. This isn't apt to be in your bailiwick anyway. I'm calling from Denver now and I'm pretty sure it ties in with monkey business up here. But I'll make you a promise. If it spills over into your bailiwick, you'll be the first to know. Okay?"

I hung up and went back to the car.

"Are you game for a trip up to Piñon Point? I'd like to find the Castle property and poke around a bit."

"What good would that do?" Holly asked a little dubiously.

"You never know. I'd like to give it a try, anyway. Are you hungry?"

"No, I had breakfast late."

It was now a little after two and Mrs. Mabie's cinnamon rolls had worn off. But it would take us an hour or so to get up there and I didn't want to arrive too late in the afternoon. It gets cold and dark rather early up in the high places. The feed bag could wait, I decided.

We headed for the hills and reached Piñon Point by three. It was half a mile off the main highway, population 375, and making a valiant effort to be a resort town. The Flapjack Bar and Restaurant had a sprinkling of tourist cars in front; there was a new motel and an ambitious peeled-log souvenir and gift shoppe. I stopped at a filling station to make inquiries. The Castle property was still unsold, according to the attendant, though a realtor had come along with a prospective buyer several times.

"You looking to buy?"

"Looking, anyway."

He told me how to find it and we headed out. The road climbed steeply, north and west from the town—a decent gravel road, but one long series of switchbacks and pretty narrow for comfort.

"How about a drunk weaving down this?" I asked.

"It's a wonder he lived to get it the way he did," Holly commented. She was keeping her eyes straight ahead; some of the drops off the right edge were a bit unnerving. Most of the turnoffs were to the left, serving ranches or other hideaway cabins, rough lanes winding away and quickly lost among the trees.

The Castle place was no exception. We found it, turned in. It was obvious no one was visiting the property much these days. Grass and weeds had grown high between the wheel ruts, untrimmed brush whipped at the sides of the car as I jockeyed along what was hardly more than a trail snaking deep into stands of pine and aspen. Quarter of a mile of it, probably; then the trees thinned out at the edge of a large clearing.

I turned the car and cut the engine. It was beautifully still. We got out and walked over to the remnants of the cabin. The foundation had been shallow, and brush had shot up thickly among the tumble of stones from the half-collapsed fireplace chimney and the odd bits of blackened and mangled metal that half filled the hole.

"If places could talk," I mused. "If they could tell you what happened."

Holly nodded, turning slowly to look around. "It's such a lovely place," she said. "So peaceful."

It was. The wind soughed gently in the tall pines surrounding the clearing, a squirrel chattered at us from a tree, streaks of late-afternoon sunlight, finding their way through passes, fell in long yellow ribbons between the trunks of the pines.

"Do I hear water?" I asked.

"Yes, I think so. There's a path into the woods over there. Let's go look."

The narrow path, carpeted with pine needles, wound away down a gentle slope for only a short distance before we came on the stream. A very small one, clear cold water tumbling down a gully over rocks.

"Why didn't we think to bring a loaf of bread and a jug of wine?" Holly asked.

"Thou, beside me in the wilderness, is good enow," I said. "Shall we walk on down a ways?"

The path was well worn, easy walking. Presently the water was singing lightly over gravel beds, only occasionally breaking into louder music where it swirled around stones. We found a boulder just off the path and sat down to smoke before starting back. We might have been a million miles from civilization; there was only the subdued sound of the water here and the wind in an aspen grove behind us.

"It's sad to think that the best he could do with a place like this was use it for weekend drunks," I said.

"Perhaps he used it for other purposes, too. For instance, wouldn't you find it an ideal place to bring a ladylove for a weekend?"

"Oh, definitely. You're still thinking about la Parker, aren't you?—who claimed she didn't know exactly how to find the place."

"Which could have been sand in our eyes. I think we should keep her in mind, Phil."

I slid an arm around her shoulder. "Don't worry. I've got her in mind. It's just that for the moment she's sharing quarters. Okay?"

She turned and gave me a small smile.

"You have beautiful eyes," I said. "Lovely hair, a superb figure—and you are much in my mind. Suppose I used this lonely place to take advantage of you?"

Her eyes waited, gleaming a little wickedly. I drew her into my arms and kissed her. Her mouth was soft and warm; her arms slid up around my neck.

"You're rather sweet," she murmured. And then she jerked away. "What's *that?*"

That had been a sudden vigorous scratching and rustling of dry leaves up in the grove behind us.

"Some animal digging," I said, endeavoring to draw her back.

"It sounded like somebody walking around."

"Couldn't be." But the noise was louder now. Reluctantly I released her and stood up. "I'll go take a look."

She rose hastily, dropped her cigarette and stepped on it. "Not without me you won't."

We started up the slope with no chance of being quiet about it. Heavy drifts of loose leaves and bits of rotting branches and twigs crackled under our feet. Up ahead the noise abruptly stopped. I went on anyway, curious now, drawing Holly along behind me. There was another vigorous rustling of leaves and something brown and furry scuttled away among the trees. Whatever it was, we'd scared it off. The ground was leveler here and the trees were sparser. I could see where the animal had clawed away a lot of leaves, and sprays of fresh dirt were scattered beside a rough hole about a foot deep. Not too far away there was another hole with its little pile of dirt. I'm no Boy Scout, but I do know that an animal doesn't dig out two ends to its tunnel before it makes the tunnel, and neither opening had the telltale hole on down into the earth.

"Here's another," Holly said. "What in the world is it doing?"

"There's something down there it wants," I said.

"Like what?"

I didn't answer, but picked up a stick and knelt down and poked at the exposed edges of one of the holes. The earth crumbled easily, much too easily. I cleared another nearby spot of leaves and small stones and began prodding there. Again the soil was soft and loose.

I stood up. Holly hadn't said another word, was just looking at me, a curious strained expression on her face.

"Are you getting the same vibes I'm getting?" I asked.

"I—I guess so. . . ." She swallowed hard.

I searched around and found a fallen branch with some twigs still intact. It would serve as a clumsy rake. I started raking more leaves away, all around the vicinity of the holes. I kept working until I had it exposed—a faint grave-sized depression in the dirt.

"That's that," I said, dropping the branch. My voice sounded funny to myself, too thin and hollow.

Holly stumbled over to me and clutched my arm. "Something's buried there—"

"Someone's buried there," I corrected grimly.

"B-Ben Manning?"

"I suppose we shouldn't jump to conclusions, but I wouldn't say it couldn't be him."

"Oh, God . . . What'll we do, Phil?" She was suddenly pale to the lips.

"There's nothing we can do. Except get back to Piñon Point and notify the sheriff's office. I think that's over at West Bend, not too far from here, but phoning would probably be easier." I kept staring down at the depression I'd uncovered, as if staring long enough would make it go away.

"Oh, God. . . ." she said again. "Why did we ever come up here?"

I roused then, picked up the stick again, tied my handkerchief to it, and planted the stick in the soft soil. Then I took Holly's arm and hustled her down the slope to the stream. "Do you have a handkerchief?" I asked.

She hadn't—only Kleenex. But she came up with a gauzy pale-blue scarf, and I tied that to a branch. It would do as a marker of sorts to help the sheriff's posse that was going to have to come in here. We started back, walking rapidly now. The place no longer seemed attractive; even the quiet had something vaguely sinister about it. All in our minds, of course; nothing had really changed. Except the temperature, for with the last rays of sun gone over the ranges, it was turning chilly fast.

"T-turn the heater on," Holly pleaded as I got the car started. "I'm f-freezing."

"I'll give you my jacket."

"N-no. I'll be all right as soon as the heat starts. Let's just get out of here. I wish we'd never come."

"I didn't need it myself. But we were looking for answers. I think we found one."

We jounced back through the woods toward the main road, Holly huddled beside me, smoking nervously. "The thing is," she said mournfully, "that it's suddenly all real. It was just—just a wild guess before—that he might be dead. But now it isn't. He *is* dead—he's buried back there in those woods."

"We're not completely certain it's him," I said.

"It would be one awful big coincidence if it isn't him."

"Yes. Still—" I couldn't think of anything very comforting to say, so I let it go. I felt sure it was Manning. My mind had left that and moved on to other problems. By rights, I should stay here until a sheriff's posse arrived, even take them in there. If I identified myself when I phoned I'd be ordered to do exactly that, especially since Holly might be able to identify him. We'd be stuck here most of the night. It would hit the morning papers. For, regardless of what the truth was concerning Dr. Castle, this would be murder—murder that tied in somehow with the Castle case.

And somebody would have enough advance warning to take cover.

In view of that, should I report it? As an attorney, I couldn't plead ignorance for failing to report it, or failing to identify myself when I did. I could be in a nice jam if that filling-station attendant remembered us inquiring there, and he probably would.

So—what to do?

I still hadn't made up my mind by the time we reached Piñon Point. We went into the Flapjack Bar and Restaurant for coffee, and I ordered a sandwich. Holly just shook her head at the suggestion of food. She looked quite ill. I took her hand across the table.

"Look, you mustn't be so upset about this."

"But I feel as if—as if it's my fault. I sent him out here to find Ted. And he tried and this is the way it ended up for him. I feel like a murderer."

"That's nonsense."

She wasn't comforted. The coffee came and she gulped a little down.

"It's fuzz from here on in, isn't it?" she asked.

"I've been trying to make up my mind. I should report it.

But he's been up there like six weeks now. Would another twenty-four hours make any real difference?"

She stared at me.

"It would break everything open," I went on. "And somebody who feels safe at the moment could panic and take measures to escape. Right?"

"Yes—yes, that's true."

"While another twenty-four hours might give us a chance at the rest of the answers we need."

She nodded heavily. "Then—why don't we just wait? You're right, it can't make very much difference."

The waitress came with my sandwich. "You sure you won't eat something?" I urged. "You should."

"No, I—I feel too woozy, Phil. Chilled and—sort of sick. You go ahead. Then let's get back."

I wolfed my sandwich and went into the bar and bought a fifth of Scotch. Then we headed back down to Denver. She huddled beside me, silent now, eyes closed. My mind was pushing it this way and that way, but I kept still, thinking she might be asleep, until we were pulling into Denver.

"How do you feel?" I asked.

She roused. "Like bloody hell. Why?"

"I was thinking there's one thing I'd like to do right now. See Mavis Castle."

"And spring this on her?"

"It might be worthwhile to see how she reacts."

"If she and Rainier killed him would they be idiotic enough to bury him up there on her own property?"

"What safer place, if you intended to keep the property?"

"That filling-station attendant said a realtor had brought a couple of prospective buyers up there."

"That could be window dressing. If it ever came to somebody actually deciding to buy it, she could change her mind. I noticed the property was posted against hunters, too. Do you realize how long that body could have rested in peace up there if we hadn't bumbled along?"

"All right, let's go see her."

I swung around and headed over to North Hancock. But I could have spared myself the trouble. Mavis Castle's half of the duplex was dark.

"Well, that's that," I said. "So we'd better just get you home. Maybe you're coming down with a cold, the way you seem to feel. You could have picked up Irene Parker's germs."

She nodded dolefully. "I'm afraid I have. Terrible headache and kind of a scratchy throat. Speaking of her, I guess I was wrong. I don't see her dragging a man's body in there and digging that grave."

"She's a big woman. It wouldn't be impossible. I'm leaving her on my list."

We were back in Astoria by seven. I took her straight to her motel and gave her the fifth of Scotch.

"Try a few jolts. Anything else I could get for you or do? Like some Vicks for a chest rub?" I asked hopefully.

She managed a wobbly smile. "Thanks anyway. I think a hot shower and some of this good stuff and ten hours in bed will do. You'll call me in the morning?"

I nodded, drawing her into my arms again, kissing her gently. That was the way I was beginning to feel. Protective. Inclined to save her from myself. Step number one toward the ranch-house mortgage and the stork circuit. And the trouble is that at this stage you're too besotted to feel alarmed.

"Remember about the chain on your door," I said. "And let nobody, but nobody, in."

"You be careful, too, Phil. We're doing the same thing he was doing, and don't you forget it."

"I won't. Good night, Holly."

Back in the car, I sat for a moment thinking. I'd given myself twenty-four more hours before calling that sheriff and I shouldn't be wasting any of them; they might cost me enough in the end. It was still early and there was at least one other thing I could do tonight.

I headed over to the Lost Cause.

12

A few early regulars were loafing and rapping at the tables, but business wasn't rushing, and Nat, the spaniel-eyed bartender, was hunched over a book up at one end of the bar. He turned down the corner of a page and let it close as I approached.

"Remember me?" I asked. I'd certainly dropped enough money here to be memorable.

"Sure, man. What's on your mind?"

"Viola. I see she isn't here yet."

"She will be. Stick around."

"I'm pressed for time. Where does she live?"

He pulled off the granny shades and massaged his forehead as if I had added immeasurably to the load of pain he already carried. "You kidding? How do I know where all these cats live?"

"An old regular like Viola? You must have an idea." I reached for my wallet, found a five, put it down on the bar. "Would that help you have an idea? It's important."

The struggle was brief. He sighed and slid his paw over for the bill. "Couple blocks down and round the corner on

Twenty-third. There's a pizza parlor, dig? She's got a pad upstairs. But don't tell her who steered you. I like to keep my customers."

"That's a deal," I said.

Twenty-third was a dismal stretch of little half-dead business places; some of them had already given up the ghost. The pizza parlor and a laundry were still trying. I climbed the long littered flight of stairs beside the pizza parlor. A woman was parking a sack of garbage beside one of the half-open doors in a long dark hall that reeked of marijuana and pizza.

"You know a party called Viola?"

"Her? Over there." She pointed.

I bestowed a brisk three raps on the scarred door she had indicated. Nothing happened. I tried again and finally a bolt was shot and the door opened on a chain. She peered out with one eye that immediately went hostile.

"You again! What do you want?"

"I'd like to talk to you, Viola. In fact, I've just learned something I think you'll want to know."

"Like what?"

"It's quite a story. Why not let me come in?"

"Nothing doing. Beat it. Go away, huh?"

"This is unofficial so far," I said. "I can make it official if you'd prefer. I mean like fuzz, Viola."

She succumbed grumpily. "Okay, okay—pete's sake. The place is a mess, but come on in."

It was a mess, all right. A small loft room furnished with rummage-sale items. A rumpled double bed at the far end made that part of it a bedroom; an ancient refrigerator, a hot plate and an old-fashioned sink full of dirty dishes, a round table and three chairs made the front end a kitchen

and living room. She bolted the door behind me and waved
at the chairs.

"Have a seat," she said ungraciously. "But make this
snappy. I got a date."

She was delectable tonight in a long-sleeved sweatshirt,
shorts and bare feet. And, of course, the hair. She sat down,
too, crossing her legs, swinging one bare dirty-soled foot
impatiently. The marijuana stink was stronger in here than
it had been in the hall, but the butts in a tray near my
elbow were establishment filter-tips.

"You remember Ben Manning?" I asked.

She didn't fall for it. "*Who?*"

"That private detective who was questioning you about
Ted Wood back about six weeks ago."

"Don't get smart," she said coldly. "Nobody questioned
me about Ted Wood except you."

"So you said. I've found out since that you did rap with
him."

The one green eye showing between wings of hair narrowed nastily. "So Nat squealed. That dirty—" She broke
it off and took refuge in a large shrug of indifference.
"What's to boil water for? He bought me a drink and asked
a few questions just like you did. And I told him just what
I told you. And that's all there was to it."

"Then why did you deny it when I asked you about it?"

"I figured it was none of your business. Which it still
isn't. And why these questions? You said you had something to tell me."

I had decided I could stretch things a bit for the sake of
the reaction, so I said, "Ben Manning is dead, murdered.
His body was found today, buried up in the mountains."

The swinging bare foot stopped swinging. But only for

a moment. There was nothing slow with her mental processes. "So I did it because he asked me the same stupid questions you asked me. So go ahead, get me busted. The rent's just been raised on this dump and I couldn't care less." Pause. "What happened to him?"

That was the question I didn't need. "They're not sure yet," I improvised. "The body was in bad shape, been there over a month." I switched to safer ground. "The interesting thing is that it was found on a property belonging to the widow of Dr. Castle."

The one eye showing looked convincingly blank. "Come again?"

"Ted never mentioned this Dr. Castle he'd worked for in Denver just before he came down here?"

"Nope."

"And you never heard about this same Dr. Castle dying in a fire up at his mountain cabin back in the summer of 'sixty-eight? In July, to be exact. Right about the time Ted split, according to you."

"I told you I couldn't be exactly sure when he split. That was kind of a guess."

"Well, a couple of other interesting things," I said. "For one, this doc carried a big insurance policy, five hundred thousand double indemnity for accidental death. And when he died in this fire the body was burned beyond recognition. Of course, a badly burned body can sometimes be identified by teeth; but if the victim wore plastic dentures, that's out, and Dr. Castle wore plastic dentures. So he had to be identified by a few personal articles, ring, keys, like that. The sort of things, in short, that could be planted on the body of another man—a man who would of course have had to wear plastic dentures, too."

She shot out of her hair like a startled rabbit. *"That's why you asked me about Ted's teeth!"*

"Yes. What I'm saying is that Ted could have been the man who died in that fire. If so, it was murder and insurance fraud, of course. Maybe you see now why it's important for me to try to find out if Ted Wood was ever seen again after he split that summer."

She leaned back, visibly relaxing a little. "Well, I told you true on that, man. I never saw or heard of him again." Pause. "His wife got all that bread? This doc's wife, I mean."

"The insurance money? Yes."

"She must have been in on it, then—I mean, if it was like you said."

"Could well be."

She was shrewd. "But if the doc pulled that, he'd sure have wanted *some* of the bread?"

"That could well be, too."

"Bro-ther!" she breathed—and it was an expression of pure admiration. "Like, some operator, huh?"

"Yeah, some operator," I agreed. Then I leaned across the table toward her. "You're sure Ted split the way you said he did?"

"Of course I'm sure. How many times do I have to tell you that?"

"But suppose he didn't. Or suppose he'd told you all about this Dr. Castle."

"But he didn't."

"Maybe you're lying, Viola. Let's spell it out carefully. Let's say Dr. Castle needed a body and he remembered this hippie drifter who'd worked for him once. He came down here and found Ted and asked him to come back up to

Denver again, maybe promised him a job or something. Then got him up to that cabin and drugged him or something and planted the identifying articles on him, and sprinkled the gasoline and cleared out for Mexico or Canada."

She parted the hair to glare at me. "Okay, okay, even if he did, what's that got to do with me?"

"You could have known that Ted went up there and never returned. And then you read in the paper about the doc dying in that fire and you're smart enough to figure out what might have happened. You know the widow will be collecting all that nice insurance money and you have a good hunch she isn't a widow at all. Now, what would any normal greedy grasping girl do in a situation like that?"

She bolted to her feet. "Listen, you crummy shyster, don't you start trying to make trouble for me."

"No trouble, Viola. I'm not accusing you, just investigating possibilities. You'll have to admit that's one. On the other hand, I'll have to admit it's pretty improbable."

She was trembling with rage. "You just bet your sweet life it's pretty improbable, man."

"Okay, okay—I wanted to see how you'd react. You've convinced me. Sit down."

"The hell with that. I've listened to enough of this crap. Take your lousy possibilities and get the hell out of here."

"Oh, come on—cool it. Unless you want me dragging the fuzz in on this."

"Fuzz" was the magic word. She got hold of herself with an effort and sat down.

"One more little question," I said. "Why'd you send that hippie over to Miss Wood's motel to rough her up?"

"I don't know what you're talking about."

"It had to be you. You picked up a packet of motel

matches that were lying on the table while we rapped at the
Lost Cause. There wasn't another person we'd seen all day
who knew where she was staying."

Her silence was flat and sullen.

"All right, clam up if you want to," I said. "It doesn't
change anything. It had to be you and there had to be a
reason. The only reason I can think of is that you didn't
want us poking into Ted's disappearance, and the only reason you'd care whether or not we poke is because you know
more than you're admitting. Right?"

"Wrong," she snapped.

"So have it your way," I sighed, and shoved to my feet.
I looked around. "Some pad you've got here. You like it?"

"That's my business."

"I'll have to admit that if you'd been doing a spot of extortion you'd be able to live better than this. Unless——" I
reached out and grabbed her wrist and hauled her to her
feet. "Let's roll up the sleeve, Viola."

No maiden ever fought harder for her virtue. She twisted
and clawed at me, but I got the sweatshirt sleeve pushed
up above her elbow. It was an ugly sight. I let go of her and
she sank into the chair and put her head down on the table.
I felt a little sick.

"What does it cost, Viola? Fifty, seventy a day—maybe
even more?"

"I kicked it," she said thickly. "A long time ago."

"How dumb do you think I am? Where do you get the
kind of bread it takes for smack?"

She raised her head and lashed out at me. "How do most
women get the bread, stupid? Will you get out of here now?"

"Okay," I said wearily.

I left her, descended the stairs and went back to where

I'd left my car. Heading home, I still felt sick. The junkies, suspended precariously between their two hells, depress me as nothing else can. And hustling for it on Cherokee Street didn't sweeten the picture. If that's what she was doing. She hadn't convinced me. Nothing she'd said had convinced me.

I garaged the car and climbed the stairs to my apartment. The phone was ringing as I let myself in. I went over and picked it up.

"Mr. Kramer, this is Mavis Castle."

"Yes, Mrs. Castle?"

"I tried to see you at your office this afternoon. The girl said—"

"Yes, I was gone all afternoon. I'm sorry. Where are you now?"

She was at a drugstore up the street. "I've got to talk to you, Mr. Kramer."

"All right. Come on along. Just ring downstairs and I'll let you in. I'm two RE."

So the day wasn't quite over. I went to fix myself a Scotch.

13

IT DIDN'T take her long. She rang from downstairs and I pressed the buzzer button and a minute later she was at the door.

"I know this is an imposition, coming to your apartment," she said.

"Not at all. I'm happy to see you. Let me take your jacket."

"Thank you—" She was obviously tense and nervous, covering it with a kind of mechanical politeness. She slipped out of the jacket. "Just toss it here—anywhere. I'll try not to be long about this."

"It's early, don't worry. Drink?"

"No—no, thank you."

"I'm having a Scotch. You'd better join me." She looked as if she could use one.

She succumbed. "All right, I will."

She was killing a half-smoked cigarette in an ashtray when I came back from the kitchen with her drink. I'd already decided to keep still about my trip up to her property until I'd heard what was on her mind. I watched her take a small sip of the drink and set the glass down. She didn't seem to know where to start.

"Leslie would kill me if he knew I was here."

"Then we'll hope he doesn't find out," I said cheerfully.

She drew a long unsteady breath, then plunged. "I—I've got to ask you to help me, Mr. Kramer. I'm at the end of my rope. I need advice. This is business, you understand. I mean, I've come to you as an attorney. I expect to pay for your help."

"All right, if that's how you want it, Mrs. Castle, though I'd be happy to help anyway. But let's have it. What's your problem?"

"You remember what you said to me day before yesterday? About the possibility of my husband still being alive?"

"Yes."

"Suppose it's true. Suppose David did plot an insurance swindle and used the body of another man in that fire."

To say that my interest quickened would be putting it mildly. "Well? Did he, Mrs. Castle?"

Her eyes met mine with an accusing bitterness. "No, you answer me first. Suppose it's true. It will be assumed that I was a party to it, won't it? No one will ever believe that I didn't know, wasn't an accomplice. Even you, when you spoke of it, insinuated that much."

"Wait a minute," I said. "Your being an accomplice is one probability, of course—and by far the easiest to assume. But let me assure you that I, for one, can believe you were totally ignorant of what was going on. The trouble is—"

"Yes?"

"The trouble is that if you've found out since that it was an insurance swindle—as obviously you must have, since you're talking in these terms—it was your duty to go to the police. And, of course, if you've turned money over to him, then I'm afraid you've put yourself in the position of accessory."

She said in a tone of desperation, "But if I don't *really* know—if I just have reason to suspect it might be true—and have been paying out money not to him, but to someone who claims he's alive—"

"That begins to sound like quite a different kettle of fish," I said. "But suppose we start at the beginning, Mrs. Castle, and you tell me exactly what has happened. I honestly can't express an opinion until I hear the details."

She seized her drink, took a couple of quick swallows, set it down again, knotted her hands tightly in her lap.

"It started right after the insurance company settled the claim with me, and that was almost a year after David died. You understand the investigation was a long and—and careful one. Anyway, it was around the end of May 1969 that I received the money. And one night, possibly a few weeks later, a woman phoned me. She did not identify herself and it was not a voice I recognized. She told me David was alive and in Canada, that he was desperately ill, needed money and had sent her to appeal to me for help. There was nothing sinister or—or threatening about it. She made it sound very much like what it purported to be, the kind of appeal for help that might have come from David himself." She paused. "You can imagine the kind of shock it was."

I nodded. "Indeed I can. And I take it you believed her?"

"At first, no. I said it was impossible. Then she told me how it had been done—how David had secured another body and planted it in the cabin. She explained that he had wanted to go away, start over somewhere else, but he had also wanted to provide for me. Arranging it so I could collect that insurance money had seemed the only way. If he hadn't become ill, he would not be asking me for any of the money, would never have risked exposing the fact that he was still alive—even to me." Mavis Castle broke off, lifted one hand in a sharp little gesture. "By then I was beginning to believe her. Maybe I was a terrible fool to swallow it. But she made it sound so convincing."

"So what did you tell her?"

"I said I had to have time to think. I asked her to call me again the following night. Then I went to Leslie, of course. He refused to believe it. He said it was some kind of an extortion attempt. When the woman called the next night he talked to her and got tough. Then she put the pressure on, said pay up or she'd expose the fact that David was alive. Leslie told her to go ahead, we didn't care whether we lost the insurance money or not. She said we'd care when I went to prison as David's accomplice and there would be evidence to prove I had known what he was doing and helped him do it." She paused, then lifted anguished eyes to mine. "You see?"

"I see," I said grimly. "And I suppose the scare tactics worked."

"Can you blame us, Mr. Kramer? We were frightened. We knew nothing. We could only guess and flounder. At first Leslie said that her threats were meaningless, because if David were really alive he'd be as vulnerable as we were. But then we realized that if he were in Canada, as she claimed, in hiding and almost certainly living under a different name, *he* could be safe enough. While we—or I, at least, would be the one in trouble."

I leaned forward and looked at her intently. "Were you able to believe, Mrs. Castle, that your husband could pull a thing like that on you? Be vindictive enough to implicate you just because you wouldn't play ball over the money?"

She picked up her glass again, but without raising it to her lips. A little pulse began to beat rapidly in her temple.

"How can I answer that?" she asked miserably. "In my heart, I suppose not. Yet our marriage had gone very bad. There was—a lot of ill feeling on both sides. I suppose it's difficult to believe that someone you once loved and who once loved you could be so cruel—so vindictive, as you put it. But I had to face the fact that it was possible. He—he had done so many things over the years that I once wouldn't have believed possible. The drinking, the women—" She broke off and stared down at the glass in her hands. "Anyway, even if I found it hard to believe David would do such a thing to me, there was this woman. For all I knew, she might have been fully capable of doing it."

"Did you have any idea at all of who she might be?"

"None—none whatsoever. I assumed she must be living with him, may have been some woman from his past, but not necessarily so, of course."

"These weren't long-distance calls?"

"No, we did learn that much. The calls were apparently made right there in Denver. But that proved nothing, either, since she had been sent to get the money."

"And she got it?"

She nodded dully. "Yes. We agonized for another twenty-four hours and finally we decided to play ball. She was asking for fifty thousand dollars. We said we'd pay. It was a mistake, of course—a serious mistake."

"How was the transaction arranged?"

"I was ordered to get the money in hundred-dollar bills and put them in a soft briefcase. Then to drive out in the country south of Denver to a certain bridge over a dry gulch on a little country road. I stop on the bridge and throw the briefcase over the railing into the gulch. It's a flat treeless area; you can see in every direction, there's no cover at all.

Almost no traffic on the road. Then I drive away. That's all."

I picked up my glass. It was empty. "I'm going to have another. Can I freshen yours?"

"No, thank you."

She was sitting hunched over with her head in her hands, a picture of desolation, when I came back.

I sat down and said, "Well, I'm sure you heard from her again."

"Yes, in about six months. She called again and wanted another fifty thousand. What could we do? By succumbing the first time we'd put ourselves in a hopeless position and we knew it. There was nothing to do but pay."

"It was the same woman?"

"Yes, without question."

"And it happened yet again?"

"Last January, yes—again. The same woman, the same amount."

"Did you at any time ask her for some proof that David was alive?"

"Indeed I did—right from the start. But she said that if she were to give me evidence of that kind I could use it to double-cross David and try to exonerate myself. I told her I would settle for hearing his voice, which was hardly anything I could take to the police as evidence. She said *they* couldn't risk that—that it might be a trap, that we could have the police listening in. In short, no matter what I suggested she insisted it would be too dangerous for them. And given everything, I suppose it would have been. So that I couldn't conclude she was lying about David on the basis of her refusal to give me proof."

She reached for a cigarette. I lit it for her and one for

myself, then rose and took a turn or two around the room.

"Mrs. Castle," I came back to where she sat. "Tell me honestly. Do you believe your husband is alive?"

She shook her head in a kind of slow numb way. "I—I just don't know, Mr. Kramer. Sometimes I think he may be, sometimes I feel sure he can't be. It's awful. I think of it all the time and I can't be sure. I just get more and more confused. I only—torture myself over it. Even Leslie has moments when he thinks it may be true. But we know this much now: whether it's true or not, we're trapped."

"You are absolutely sure you do not recognize the voice of the woman who calls?"

"I am positive. Don't you think I've racked my mind over that?"

"Does the voice, the manner of speaking, give you any idea of the kind of woman she might be? Educated or not? Some particular ethnic background? Is there an accent, peculiar inflections or words?"

She thought a minute. "No, it's just an ordinary voice. She says as little as possible, she's brisk and businesslike. Now and then I've gotten an impression that she—well, that she has been carefully drilled."

"Rather rotelike, you mean?"

She nodded.

"Tell me something else. Did you ever know a woman called Virginia Logan who was supposed to be involved with your husband at the time he died?"

"I knew about her, but I didn't know her. I'd long ago given up being curious about the women in his life."

"Never heard her voice on the phone?"

She hesitated. "Oh, it's possible I did, but if so I don't remember it. And anyway this woman was thoroughly checked out by the insurance investigators. They learned about her and David, you know. They watched her for a long time. She had gone back to Michigan by then, something about her mother being ill, but they watched her."

I sank into my chair again. "If he *is* alive, it's simple enough: the woman is operating with him, for him. But if he is not alive, then it almost has to be some woman who knew him and all the circumstances surrounding his death well enough to have dreamed up what appears to be quite a clever extortion plot. That wouldn't necessarily be Virginia Logan, of course. Could be some other woman dating further back."

Irene Parker flashed into my mind. I mulled it for a moment. Then I said, "Mrs. Castle, what made you suddenly decide to come and tell me all this?"

"Because it's happened again," she cried. "She called me late yesterday. Fifty thousand again, to be taken to the same place. And last night Leslie went berserk when I told him. He's determined to be there waiting for her. I've got to stop him, but he won't listen to me."

She slid forward, fastening anxiety-haunted eyes on me. "He knows there's no cover and he knows it may not be a woman who comes to pick up the money. He knows there could be two or more of them. He knows he could be killed. But he's beyond caring. It does that to you, poisons and sickens you to the point where you can't exercise judgment, can't *think* at all. I don't know if you can understand that, but—"

"I can understand it," I said grimly. "I think I'd react the same way. When do you take the money there?"

"Tomorrow night at eight o'clock."

"By daylight?"

"If they actually watch me—and she says I'm under constant surveillance—it would have to be by daylight, wouldn't it? Anyway, it always has been."

"And exactly what does Leslie plan to do?"

"He thinks they wouldn't be watching much ahead of time, especially now that it has worked on three previous occasions and they feel confident about us. So he intends to go out there late in the afternoon. Oh, not to the spot itself. But he has explored the vicinity and found a wood lot about a mile up the gulch from the bridge. He thinks he can hide his car there and work his way down the gulch to the bridge."

"And wait under the bridge for the pickup."

She nodded miserably. "With—with a gun. That's what frightens me so, Mr. Kramer. He thinks he can capture them. But you know as well as I do what little chance he'd have. And if something goes wrong, he'll kill, I know he will —or be killed. That's why I'm here. I hoped—I hoped you could do something to stop him. Listen—" she slid forward on the chair again—"I'm ready to blow everything before I'll let him do this. I'll go to the police, if it's the only way. I'll confess and take the consequences. Anything—anything. There's no use in going on like this, anyway. We don't have a life. We don't have anything but fear and worry. I love Leslie, but we can't marry so long as there's a possibility that David is alive. What is there for us to—to save?"

Her voice broke on a dry sob of despair and she covered her face with her hands. I leaned over and gripped her shoulder.

"Don't, Mrs. Castle. Easy does it, now. We'll work this out. You have the money?"

She got control of herself, raised her face. "Yes, I've arranged to pick it up from the banks in the morning. I've scattered the money, you see—with this hanging over me, it seemed safer to never make large withdrawals at any one place."

"And where is Leslie now?"

"Home, I suppose, at his apartment." She sucked in a huge breath. "You'll do something—to stop him?"

"I don't know that he should be stopped."

She stared at me, dismayed. "But—"

"Look." I leaned over and took her hand. "I know how you feel. But the thing I'd like to do is talk Leslie into letting me go with him. Two of us could have a chance. And I'll carry the gun, so that he can't do too much damage even if he loses his head."

She went on staring at me, uncertain, still frightened.

"It could be the only way to solve this thing, Mrs. Castle, and too good an opportunity to pass up. You can see that yourself, can't you? So the thing for you to decide is whether you think you can persuade Leslie yourself or want me to go up there and talk to him."

"I—I don't know what to say. He'll be furious at me for coming to you."

"Sure, he'll fume around at first—but he'll get over it. If he has half the brains I think he has, he knows this thing has to come to a head in more ways than one. He loves you, he wants to marry you, doesn't he?"

"Yes—"

"Then this question of your husband being alive has to be resolved for once and for all. If he is alive, we'll worry about getting you out of an accessory charge when we know. And if he isn't, you've got to know that too, beyond any shadow of a doubt, or you'll never have a life worth living. Right?"

She nodded numbly.

"Can you talk to Leslie tonight? Do your best to persuade him?"

"I'll try," she said.

"One other thing. If he'll go along with this, don't pick up the money. Stuff some newspapers into a briefcase, make it about the right heft. You understand?"

"Yes."

"I'll be coming up to Denver in the morning and I'll check in with you. If he proves stubborn there'll still be time for me to talk to him." I hesitated, then decided to mention it. "By the way, Mrs. Castle. I went to see Rufus Langley this morning."

"Rufus?" She looked bewildered. "But why? He can't really know anything about all this."

"Well, there's one thing he certainly thinks he knows. That the typewriter found in the debris of the fire belonged to him."

"Oh, that. Yes, it's true. David may have taken it to a repair shop and picked it up before he went to the cabin. But it's even more likely that he had forgotten to take it to the repair shop at all. In any case, it must have been in his car when he went up there."

"I understand he sometimes worked on medical papers at the cabin."

"Yes, so he must have remembered he had it in the car and decided to use it."

"Suppose he'd forgotten to take it to the repair shop, though. Why would he have taken it into the cabin then?"

"He liked to tinker with mechanical things. Probably thought he could fix it." She hesitated. "You know, Rufus gets very confused about things. One-track mind and all that."

I nodded. "You realize he has a big down on you?"

"He dislikes me intensely," she said simply. "It used to bother me greatly. But David said he disliked all women and it wouldn't have mattered whom he married, Rufus would have disapproved. So I—I've learned to live with it."

"What time," I asked, "did David go up to the cabin that Friday?"

"Right after lunch. He came home for that at noon, left around one-thirty."

"All right," I said, and rose to get her jacket. She slipped into it and picked up her purse. She still looked white and very exhausted, which was natural enough. She'd been through a lot. But she seemed much calmer.

"Do your best with Leslie," I said. "And I'll see you in the morning."

I went out to the kitchen when she'd gone and fixed myself a sandwich, having missed dinner in the day's shuffle. I thought about Mavis Castle as I sat munching the sandwich at the kitchen table. Attractive, intelligent, appealing. But a lady in real distress? Or a lady carefully setting me up for a snow job because she realized the truth could not be kept under wraps much longer? I didn't know. Any more than I knew why I'd decided to keep still about that grave I'd found up on the Castle property. It seemed to me that if I'd trusted her thoroughly I would have told her about it. Because the first place the fuzz were going, once they'd dug up that body, was straight to her.

I finished my sandwich, topped it off with a nightcap and went to bed.

14

FIRST ORDER of business in the morning was a call to Jerry Howe at Homicide. His check on Virginia Logan had been fruitful up to a point. The lady had unquestionably spent a little over a year—from May 1968 to June 1969—in Arlington, Michigan, a town of some thirty thousand. During this time the Arlington police had quietly kept an eye on her, apparently at the request of the insurance company. Her mother had died in December; she had then spent some months settling decedent's business affairs and selling the family home. And finally departed for Cleveland in June. Arlington police had no further knowledge of her, of course.

It was fairly safe to assume, I decided, that surveillance might have followed her for a while, just to make sure; in which case one had also to assume that she had committed no indiscretion like joining Dr. Castle—or reasonable facsimile thereof. Still, it left a lot of questions. Could she and Dr. Castle have played it so carefully and coolly that they had gone separate ways for several years to discourage suspicion? Or was I off on the wrong track entirely? Was Dr. Castle really dead and someone out to take the widow by making her believe he was alive? And if so, was it the Logan woman—or someone else from his apparently large list of ladyloves? Last, but not leastly, was the widow leading me up a creek with her story of extortion, and was the money going to Dr. Castle according to a plan he had hatched and executed with or without her connivance?

And even more lastly and less leastly, what *had* happened to Ted Wood?

The phone broke in on my thoughts. I picked it up and Holly said forlornly, "It's be."

I groaned. "You don't sound so good."

"I'be nod. You should see be."

"I can. You are delectable in a filmy nightgown, and a slight redness around the nose is scarcely noticeable."

"Hah! By eyes are wadering and all puffed up, and—and —and—" Three gasps ended in a sneeze.

"*Gesundheit!*" I offered fervently.

"I'be sorry. I couldn't stob id."

"Look, why don't you crawl back in the hay for the day?"

"I was thinking of it byself. I feel so awful. Ebcept I'be anxious to ged on with things. Is there anything new?"

"Nothing that can't wait until I see you. And I've decided to go up to Denver and try to find the repair shop where Dr. Castle left that typewriter of Rufus Langley's. It will probably be slow dull work, so you won't be missing a thing."

"Then maybe I'll just dake some bore asbirin and dry to sleeb."

"Fine, and I'll call you later. Maybe you'll feel like dinner by tonight. Okay?"

I hung up just as Mickey tapped on the door, then stuck her head in. "There's a man here to see you, Phil." She stepped inside, closed the door and rolled her eyes. "Wow! He's a hippie. Says his name is Conrad Baker. What would he want?"

"We could always find out," I said, "if you would merely show him in."

She showed him in. Daddy Baker had donned an ordinary sport shirt and slacks for this excursion into the establishment camp, but hair, beard, sandals and dark shades kept him on the spectacular side. I rose and shook hands.

"How are you, Mr. Baker?"

"Down here on business, so thought I'd drop by and kill two birds with one stone." He settled his bulk into the client's chair. "I told you I'd ask a few questions about Ted Wood," he continued. "So I did, and I have a little information that may interest you."

"Good."

"A chick who came up from Taos about three months ago said she had known Ted Wood there, he was living in one of the communes. It's not an uncommon name, I suppose, but I gave her the description you gave me and she said it fit."

"Did she know anything about him?"

"Just that he had come down there from Haight-Ashbury."

"Nothing as to whether he had ever been in this area?"

"No. And, of course, he may have split after the chick did. So I realize it's not much to go on. Still, I thought you'd want to know." He paused and stroked his beard. "You did say you'd checked out the Spaight Street area."

"Yes, I started there and learned that he had apparently gone back to Haight-Ashbury three years ago."

"Well, I'll tell you, Mr. Kramer. If you care to go down

to Taos and investigate I can give you the name of a man who can help you."

I pulled a memo pad over. "I'll take the name and see what my client wants me to do."

I duly wrote it down, along with instructions for finding this helpful party.

"He's been there for years and knows the scene," Daddy Baker assured me. "And believe me, looking for anybody in those communes down there can be like looking for a needle in a haystack. Without some inside help, I mean."

"I understand," I said. "And thanks very much, Mr. Baker."

"No sweat, man." He shoved easily to his feet. "Come out and see us again. I'd still like to show you that we've got a good thing going."

I do not believe you, Daddy Baker, I thought when he had gone. But I am interested to note that you bothered to try to con me. I wish I knew why.

I swiveled my chair around and stared out the window. Tribal solidarity was a big thing with the hippies, of course. Fuzz was common enemy to be thwarted by fair means or foul, and no reason a nosy establishment attorney shouldn't be lumped with fuzz. Ted Wood, one of their own, was being sought and that called for sand in the eyes. It *could* be no more than that.

Lee was in court this morning, so I had to take Mr. Benson Farley at nine-thirty. Mr. Benson Farley was having troubles with a renter in the upstairs apartment of his home. We discussed the possible measures to be taken and I got rid of him by ten. Then I left a few instructions with Mickey and headed up to Denver.

I judged that looking for the repair shop where Dr. Castle

might have taken his brother's typewriter could be a matter of looking for a needle in a haystack, too. But it seemed fairly reasonable to assume he might have picked a place in the vicinity of the Medical Arts Building, where he had had his office. I cruised up and down and around in that area for a while without spotting a sign of such a place. Finally I parked and decided to give it a try on foot. And almost immediately, turning down a rather seedy side street, I came onto Casey's Typewriter Sales and Repairs.

But it was closed and locked. That seemed strange at close to eleven o'clock of a weekday morning. I peered in the window alongside the door. There was a long counter on one side of a narrow aisle, display shelves for typewriters and office supplies on the other side. Lights were on and they weren't just night lights. I rattled the door again as noisily as possible, and again nothing happened.

I walked to the corner of the street, then up a ways to the alley opening that went in behind the buildings. A few cars were parked along its length, but there was no one in sight. I started down the alley, counting doors to the fifth one, which should have been the rear of the repair shop. It was; a small sign with "Casey's" lettered on it was tacked to the door. I reached for the knob, checked myself, got out my handkerchief, covered my hand before turning the knob. The door opened and I went in.

It was a long narrow workroom, tools and parts of half a dozen dismantled typewriters scattered around on workbenches, a desk, a safe, and a filing cabinet over in one corner. Drawers hung open from the desk and the cabinet; the safe was open, too.

And a man lay sprawled on the floor in front of it.

He was lying face down. I knelt and lifted him a little. He

was middle-aged, small, bald—and dead. There were two bullet holes in his chest. I felt the big muscle in his neck. He was still warm. An hour, two hours ago maybe, at the most.

I got up slowly and looked around. A wad of keys still dangled in the door, and a hat and a jacket were thrown down on one of the work benches. What had happened seemed fairly obvious. He'd come in, taken off his things and turned on the front lights before locking that back door. In that interval somebody had walked in and been waiting for him with a gun. Probably forced him to open the safe before shooting him. Burglary, of course.

Or was it?

I went into the front room, found the phone and called the police. While I waited I went back and examined the filing cabinet. One drawer contained repair record cards with customer names. I thumbed carefully through the C's. No Castle, though I found dates as far back as 1963. Then I found a section full of customer slips, carbons of which are given to the customers. The date on which the machine had been brought in for repairs was on a line at the top. At the bottom where Casey had scrawled "Paid," the date, presumably of both pickup and pay, was also scrawled in. I went through them very carefully, but again there was nothing for a Castle.

Had there ever been? Or was the little man lying there dead because somebody had wanted to remove such a slip? I could really think of no other reason for the files and desk drawers having been opened at all. Unless someone had imagined there might be some loose cash tucked away in them. It was remotely possible, of course.

A cruising squad car got there first—two Adam 12 types,

young, cool, polite, competent. I let them in the front door. They examined the body briefly, deftly investigated pockets.

"Wallet gone," one said. "Look around, Frank—it may have been rifled and thrown down somewhere." He rose and faced me. "You turned in the call?"

"Yes."

"May we see your identification?"

I produced same.

"What were you doing here, Mr. Kramer?"

"I wanted to look at typewriters. I found the place closed, but noticed the lights were on and that seemed funny. So I walked around to the back, thinking something might be wrong."

"This back door was open?"

"Yes. I covered my hand when I turned the knob. And I don't think I've touched anything."

"Did you know Mr. Casey? If that's him, and I suppose it is."

"No, I didn't know him."

"What brought you to this particular place?"

"I was walking by, noticed the sign, remembered I wanted to look at typewriters."

"Walking by on your way where?"

I sighed. Young, competent and thorough. He wasn't going to quit without a full report.

"Actually I was up here in Denver to visit a friend. I had a little time to spare, so I parked, hoping to find a café where I could get a cup of coffee. While I was looking for that I noticed Casey's sign and decided to stop."

"Okay, Mr. Kramer. You know we have to check it all out."

"Sure."

The other cop got up from examining the safe. "If he kept cash here, that's gone, too, Al."

Even I could see it was shaping up into burglary. Which didn't mean a thing. If somebody had wanted that customer slip from back in July '68 and wanted it badly enough to kill for it . . . But why kill for it? Why not just ask for it? Because Casey could have described the asker if anyone ever came snooping. Yes, that made sense. As it would have made sense to give it the appearance of burglary.

Sirens were wailing faintly in the distance.

"Look," I said. "Do you need me here any longer? I've told you what I know and you know where you can find me."

"Let's just clear it with the lieutenant," Al said pleasantly. "Won't take long, Mr. Kramer."

Ambulance, mobile lab, Police Department car. They all piled in and went to work like well-oiled machines. The officer in charge ignored me while he consulted with the M.E. over the body. I hung out an ear. Dead two to three hours, the gun probably a .32 pistol, the M.E. opined. While the photographers went to work on it, squatting to shoot from different angles, the officer came over to me.

"I'm Lieutenant Foster, Homicide."

He took me through it again, while Al wrote it all down this time. Finally he nodded.

"Could you stop in at Central Homicide and sign a statement this afternoon, Mr. Kramer? We'll try to have it ready by two o'clock. Anything more you can tell us?"

"I'm afraid not. What do you make of it, Lieutenant?"

He shrugged. "Probably some hophead after bread for a fix. It happens all the time."

A cop let me out the front door and I started back to where I'd left my car. There was a drugstore across the street, so I hied over there and went in to phone Mavis Castle. It rang so long I was about to hang up when she suddenly came on.

"Phil Kramer, Mrs. Castle."

"Yes—oh, yes—" She sounded oddly breathless.

"You talked to Leslie. How did it come out?"

"Just about the way you thought it would. He was furious at first, but then he cooled down and agreed to discuss it with you."

"Suppose you get hold of him and we meet at your place."

"Well—just a minute—"

There was a brief silence. I waited, puzzled. Then her voice again.

"All right, Mr. Kramer. Come along now, if you wish."

Maybe Rainier was there, I thought. I asked her.

"No, no, I'm alone here," she said. "But he—he's on his way."

"Oh, that's fine. I'll be along shortly, then."

I hung up, still faintly puzzled about the way she had sounded. Then I decided it wasn't too surprising, considering the strain she was under, if she seemed a little rattled or peculiar.

It was twenty to twelve and the drugstore lunch counter was handy, so I grabbed a bowl of soup and a sandwich. That took me half an hour. Then I headed out there, parked behind a green Chev at the curb in front of her place and walked up to the door. It opened as soon as I rang. One look at Mavis Castle's frozen face and I was sure again that something was wrong.

"Mrs. Castle, what is it?" I asked.

She forced a kind of a sickly smile. "Why, nothing, Mr. Kramer. I'm all right. Please come in."

I don't know how I could have anticipated it, so there was no more use in blaming myself than in blaming her for not being able to warn me. I walked in to find Rufus Langley standing in the middle of the living room with a pistol pointed at me.

15

"THERE was nothing I could do," Mavis Castle said in an agonized voice. "He held the gun on me while I talked to you."

"You just shut up," he snapped at her. "And sit down over there on the sofa."

She edged her way around to the sofa and sat.

"Now you, Mr. Kramer," he said. "Right beside her."

One look at that gun in his hand and my mind had flown to Casey sprawled dead in the workroom of his shop. One look at Rufus Langley's tense face and the glittering eyes behind the black-rimmed specs and I knew better than to challenge him. I too went carefully over to the sofa and sat.

"Mr. Langley," I said, "I don't understand this." It was the understatement of the year.

"I got nothing against you personally and I don't want to hurt you," he said. "But justice has to be done."

"I thought you were going to let me take care of all this. I promised you yesterday I would."

His face darkened. "Words! Just a lot of words, Mr. Kramer. I could see you didn't believe me any more than the rest of them had. Oh, I didn't let on, but"—he tapped the side of his head with his free hand—"I could tell it— right here. And then I knew."

"Knew what?"

"That there wasn't any use hoping anybody would help me and I'd just have to do it myself—with this." He moved the gun slightly to indicate what he meant.

Judge, jury and executioner, I thought. I stole a sidewise look at Mavis Castle. She was rigid with terror, her hands gripping the edge of the sofa cushion under her, her gaze riveted on Rufus Langley. I didn't feel a hell of a lot better myself, but I'd have to try to do something.

"Mr. Langley," I said, "you've got things all wrong. I did believe you. In fact, I've already been to that repair shop to try to find out the date the typewriter was picked up."

His jaw slackened. "You—have? When?"

"I just came from there. The man who runs it showed me the copy of a customer slip showing it was picked up on Friday morning. So obviously your brother had it in the car when he went up to the cabin Friday afternoon. That blows your whole case, Mr. Langley."

"You're lying," he snapped.

"How do you know that?"

"Because I—" He stopped, his jaw tightening again, his gaze narrowing. "I don't believe you, that's all. How would you know what shop it was?"

"You told me, Mr. Langley—don't you remember?"

Good try, but it didn't get me anywhere. He shook his head stubbornly. "I couldn't have told you. I didn't know myself. I just know what David said. And David wouldn't have lied."

"It wasn't exactly a lie, Mr. Langley. He was a very busy

man, you know, and probably it wasn't possible for him to get the typewriter down to you just then. So, more to spare your feelings than anything else, he told you it wouldn't be available until Saturday."

That had about as much chance of getting past his *idée fixe* as a .22 bullet had of getting through the rock of Gibraltar. He didn't even bother to answer, but shifted his gaze slightly to Mavis.

"What time is it now?"

She looked at her watch. "Twelve twenty-five."

"He should be here."

"Who? Leslie?" I asked.

She answered without turning her eyes to me. "Yes. He made me call him and ask him to come here. He said he thought he could make it by noon."

"Then why isn't he here?" Rufus Langley demanded suspiciously. "He's trying to pull something, isn't he?"

"He could easily have been delayed, Mr. Langley," I said. "He'll be coming and the four of us can talk things over. None of us is interested in trying to get away, so why don't you put the gun down and relax?"

He wasn't *that* balmy. Instead, he backed carefully over to the front windows and gave a quick look out.

I tried again. "Mr. Langley, when did you leave the Four Pines?"

"Never mind that."

"Last night," Mavis said quickly in a low voice. "They called me this morn—"

"You shut up," he repeated vehemently, brandishing the gun. And then almost petulantly: "What are they doing out there?"

"Who?" I asked.

"Police. That Rainier—he's pulled something." He glared at Mavis. "You told him something—you warned him somehow."

"Why don't you let me take a look, Mr. Langley?"

"You stay where you are," he snapped, but he gave another quick nervous glance out the window.

"What do they seem to be doing?" I asked.

"They're—examining the car."

"Your car, Mr. Langley?"

"He stole an employee car," Mavis said softly. "Green Chevrolet."

"I didn't *steal* it," he exclaimed indignantly. "I just used it."

"They've spotted it, Mr. Langley," I said. "And they'll be coming up here to ask questions. You're going to be in more trouble than this is worth, if you don't give up right now. Come on. Hand over the gun and we'll—"

"No you don't." He darted back into the center of the room and looked at Mavis. "Your car—it's in the garage in back. Give me the keys."

He was getting panicky, and that really scared me. I said quietly, "Go ahead, give him the keys, Mrs. Castle."

"They're in my purse. It's in the desk."

"Get them," I said.

She rose gingerly and started over to the desk.

"Wait!" Rufus Langley had seen his share of TV cops and robbers. "Which drawer? I'll get it."

"Top one, right side."

He circled around to the desk, fished out the purse, opened it and found the keys.

"All right, both of you stand up," he ordered.

Mavis was already on her feet. I rose.

"Now you, Mr. Kramer, lie down on the floor."

"What about her?"

"She's going with me."

"Don't be an idiot," I said sharply. "I'm not going to allow you to take her out of here."

He brandished the gun menacingly. "You can't stop me, Mr. Kramer. I don't want to hurt you, but I will if I have to."

"No, I don't think you'll do that," I said quietly, and I started walking toward him. "You won't do it, because I'm the only one who can help you. Listen, I found out the truth, the real truth, Mr. Langley. You were right about everything. We'll get those police in here and I'll tell them the whole story."

"You're lying to me!" he shouted, backing away. "And I'll shoot. I *will!*"

I went on moving toward him very slowly. "I wouldn't lie to you, Mr. Langley. Let me help you—"

"Get back!" he screamed.

Luck was with me. The doorbell rang at that moment and the last shred of his control snapped. He veered in a crouch and ran for the hallway that led into the kitchen. I lunged after him, literally throwing myself upon him, closing one arm around his neck, grabbing for his gun hand with the other. The gun went off and a bullet plowed into a closet door. But I had him. I wrested the gun out of his hand and hauled him back into the room and shoved him down in a chair.

Mavis had run to the door, and two squad-car men had tumbled in, followed by Leslie Rainier.

"Everything's all right," I said, turning.

Mavis was in Rainier's arms, sobbing. One of the uniformed men had drawn his service revolver.

"What the hell's going on here?" he demanded.

"It's all okay now, officer," I said. "This is the man who escaped from the sanitarium in the green Chevrolet outside. You spotted it?"

He nodded. "There was a bulletin out. What did he do?"

"Came in here and pulled a gun on the lady. I came along and he had us both cornered until I jumped him."

"Nobody's hurt?"

"No, the gun just went off when I grabbed for it. Splintered some wood in a door."

He holstered his revolver and put his hand out for the gun. "Maybe you'd better all just sit down and we'll get this straightened out," he said.

It had been my day for fuzz, I thought, as we sat and Mavis, very pale but composed now after the brief flurry of tears, told how Miss Buffington had called from the Four Pines about ten o'clock to report Rufus Langley missing since late last night. He had seized the cottage nurse when she brought in his medication, gagged her, tied her up, taken her keys. One of them had opened a drawer in her desk that contained a gun. He had taken that, left the cottage and gone down to the employee parking lot, where he'd found a car with keys in it.

"Why in the world did you let him in?" I asked her.

"I couldn't believe he would really harm me. I thought I could reason with him. But he drew the gun and ordered me to phone Leslie."

The young officer meticulously writing everything down asked, "What made him come here, ma'am?"

"He—well, he blamed me for something that had happened long ago," Mavis said. "My husband, Mr. Langley's brother, died accidentally in a fire, and Mr. Langley was convinced that I had been responsible for his death."

Rufus Langley was slumped in the chair like a sack of wet wash. But he raised his head and looked at us bitterly now. "Both of them," he cried. "They killed David. He too." He pointed at Rainier. "I can prove it. But nobody will listen to me."

The young cop nodded diplomatically. "Sure, Mr. Langley. We understand. Tell us, now, where did you go after you left the san? Where did you spend the night?"

"In some woods. I slept in the car."

The other cop had been on the phone, checking at the Four Pines and at precinct headquarters. He hung up and turned around and I walked over to him. He was the one who had the gun, and he had put it down beside the phone.

"Officer," I said, "would you examine that gun? It's been handled so much there wouldn't be any fingerprints that mattered on it. But I'd like to know if it's been fired more than once."

He picked it up, sniffed it, then sprang the mag out and counted the bullets through the small holes in the side. "Five, with the one in the mag," he said. "And it's an eight-shot automatic, thirty-two caliber." He turned around and went over to Rufus Langley. "How many times did you fire this gun, Mr. Langley?"

"I—I don't know. I practiced last night while I was hiding in those woods. It was a long time since I'd handled a gun. I don't know. I guess I fired it a couple of times."

"Where were these woods?"

He didn't know that either—just some woods somewhere between there and Astoria.

The officer looked at me. "Why are you concerned about this?"

"Let's talk in the kitchen," I said.

Out there, I told him about Casey. His gaze narrowed.

"Very interesting. I'll see that Ballistics checks it out. These nuts, you just never know what they'll do."

Back in the living room the other cop had finished asking questions. "What now, Bill?"

"The sergeant said to bring him down to the precinct station, and they'll send somebody for the car."

"You're not arresting him?" Mavis exclaimed.

"No, ma'am. Just holding him there until the people from the san can come after him. If we need further information we'll be in touch with you folks." He turned to Rufus Langley. "Now, then, sir, we'll just go along quietly, shall we?"

Rufus Langley went along quietly, without another word or look at any of us.

"Poor devil," Rainier said.

I nodded. Somehow I felt like I'd kicked my mother on Mother's Day. "I could use a drink," I said.

16

RAINIER went to the kitchen, brought back glasses and a bottle of brandy and poured.

"I guess I should be grateful to you, Kramer," he admitted grudgingly. "If Mavis had been here alone I don't like to think what might have happened."

"Obviously he wasn't going to do anything until you got here." I took a long sweet swallow of the brandy. "As for what he intended to do then, God only knows. Force a confession, commit a ritual killing—probably he didn't know himself."

"Well, he would have made a getaway with her in the car," Rainier said. "And I don't like to think about that either."

"I still don't believe Rufus would have harmed me," Mavis said. She turned to me. "Why were you asking about the gun being fired, Mr. Kramer?"

I hesitated. Keeping my own counsel might not be a bad idea. But it was tempting to see how they'd react. "As a matter of fact, Mrs. Castle," I said, "I came up here this morning to try to find the repair shop where your husband might have taken Rufus' typewriter. I found one about six blocks from the Medical Arts Building. And the little guy who ran it had been shot to death in his back room, just a few hours before I barged in."

I was watching both of them. She jerked erect in her chair, shock and incredulity in her eyes. Rainier just stared at me, his dark gaze frozen.

"I don't understand," Mavis quavered. "You mean it *was* the shop where David had taken the typewriter? And you think that Rufus had gone there and—and—"

I shrugged. "I don't know. It merely seemed reasonable to assume Dr. Castle might have picked a place near his office to have the machine fixed. I called the police, of course, and while I was waiting for them to come I examined the file contents, customer slips, et cetera. I found nothing there under Dr. Castle's name. But if Rufus, or someone else for that matter, had gotten there ahead of me there wouldn't, of course, have been anything for me to find."

"But Rufus said he didn't know what shop it was. You heard him."

"Sure, but he may have been lying. Or he may have reasoned as I did that it would be somewhere in the vicinity of Dr. Castle's office."

Rainier said evenly, "It could have been burglary or something, couldn't it?"

I sloshed the brandy around in my glass. "Very possibly. That's what the police think. The guy's wallet was gone and money may have been taken from the safe. Still, a ten-year-old coming in there to take something from the files would have been smart enough to cover by making it look like burglary."

Mavis sprang to her feet. "I don't believe it. I just don't

believe that it could have been Rufus, I mean. Why, he couldn't even bring himself to fire at you, Mr. Kramer. I can't believe he'd kill anyone."

"You're probably right, Mrs. Castle. Still, I thought it should be checked out through Ballistics. My own feeling is Rufus was so convinced the typewriter had been picked up on Saturday that it wouldn't have occurred to him that he needed proof."

"I agree with that," Rainier said. "Besides, if he had had something like a customer slip to prove his point wouldn't he have been brandishing it around?"

"Not if he'd killed to get it," I said. "Unless he's even balmier than we think." I paused, studying the brandy in my glass. "We all know what Rufus believed. That some-body picked up the typewriter Saturday afternoon and went up to the cabin with it and set that fire. Suppose he was right to the extent that the typewriter *was* picked up on Saturday. You both have an alibi for Saturday night, when the fire presumably started. But what about Saturday afternoon? Could either of you prove exactly where you were and what you were doing?"

There was a silence. Then Mavis said woodenly, "I was at Leslie's apartment all afternoon."

"Could anyone but Leslie verify that?"

Rainier answered. "No. We—were alone." He stared down into his own glass a moment or two before he added heavily, "You don't think—you don't *really* think that either of us had anything to do with that fire?"

"To be honest, Rainier," I said, "I don't know either of you well enough to be sure of anything."

Mavis turned and walked slowly to a window. I watched Rainier continue to stare glumly down at the glass in his hand. He looked rugged. There were deep furrows at the corners of his mouth, dark circles under his eyes.

Finally I said, "Well, this isn't getting us to the main order of business. Do we have a deal for tonight, Rainier?"

"We did have. Mavis fixed that. I was willing to go along, but now . . . ."

"But now?"

He looked at me levelly. "If you don't trust us, if you don't believe what she told you, why should we trust you?"

"Try it this way," I said. "If I were at all convinced that Mavis hadn't told me the truth, I certainly wouldn't be sticking my neck out to try to help you."

His jaw tightened. "I don't need any help."

Mavis turned pleadingly. "Les, please—oh, please, you promised me."

He stared at her for a moment, then dropped his gaze. "All right. We go down through Englewood on Eighty-three to Yuba. It's a country road a little north of there."

"Then suppose I meet you at Yuba. And the earlier the better, I suppose."

"I'd say we should meet by four at the latest. But why not at my office and take the one car?"

"I think I'd rather take mine too."

He shrugged consent. "I'll park somewhere along the main drag in Yuba if I get there first. You can't miss me, there's only two blocks of business district. I'm driving a light-blue Olds convertible, and I'll bring the things we need."

I turned to Mavis. "You fixed the briefcase the way I told you?"

"Yes, we did that last night."

"Is there any chance this woman might call and change your orders at the last minute?"

"It's always possible, I suppose. But she never has."

"It's a chance we'll have to take," Rainier said.

I went over and poured myself another dollop of brandy and stood sloshing that around in my glass for a moment. Then I said, "There's another thing that isn't going to make either of you feel any better. But I think I'd better tell you anyway. Yesterday Miss Wood and I went up to see the site of the cabin. We were poking around in the woods, walked down the stream a ways, and found a grave."

"A *grave!*" Rainier gaped in naked astonishment. Mavis Castle, still standing over by the windows, looked as if somebody had clubbed her and she hadn't gotten around to falling yet.

"You—can't be serious!" she gasped.

"I wish I weren't, Mrs. Castle. But there's a rough trench back there in the woods; animals, obviously attracted by the odor, have been digging in it and every indication is that a body has been buried there. My guess is that it's the body of Ben Manning, that private detective Miss Wood sent here from New York six weeks ago."

"You guess?" Rainier exclaimed. "You mean, you didn't call the police?"

"No. I decided to wait twenty-four hours and see what else I could learn before letting this particular information become public. After you came to me last night, Mrs. Castle, I was glad that I had. For if this had hit the papers by today there might have been no pickup tonight, and no opportunity to put our hands on whoever has taken you for one hundred and fifty thousand dollars."

Rainier's gaze was riveted on me. "You think that if this

Manning had been killed, and if that's his body up there, these extortionists are the killers?"

"It could be a fair assumption," I said. "The thing is—" I looked at my watch—"I'm just about due to make that call to the sheriff. Once the machinery is in motion it may take them three to four hours to get in there and bring the body out. Then they'll be coming to you, Mrs. Castle, since it's your property."

She sank into a chair and covered her face with her hands. "Oh, God!" she said in a stricken voice.

"But," I continued, "there's also a faint chance they may contact you as soon as they get my call. That won't do. It could tie you up and keep you from driving out there with the briefcase. Is there a place where you could go and stay until it's time for you to leave?"

"She can go to my apartment," Rainier said.

"Then I'd suggest you do that. It will serve another purpose too. If the woman makes an attempt to call and change orders at the last minute she'll be out of luck." I downed the brandy left in my glass and set the glass on a table. "Needless to say, I'm depending on you to keep your mouth shut about who tipped off the sheriff's office. The law wouldn't take kindly to my twenty-four-hour delay."

Rainier had gone to put his arms around her shoulder. "You can trust us," he said.

"Good. Now I've got things to do, so I'll beat it. Yuba— four o'clock."

When I got over to Central Homicide a little past two the statement wasn't ready. I had to cool my heels for half an hour before I was taken into Lieutenant Foster's office. I read the statement over and it sounded okay and I couldn't think of anything to add to it, so I signed.

"Any ballistic report yet?" I asked.

"No, we're still waiting. One of the precinct stations sent a gun over to be checked. Some nut who had escaped from a mental institution had been waving it around. But we probably won't hear for a couple hours yet."

"Anything else new on the case?"

"I wish to God there were," he sighed. "You take this kind of a job, if it's the kind of a job I think it is, and they're the hardest thing in the world to crack. Some faceless creep drifts in and drifts out again and there's nothing to get hold of, absolutely nothing."

"Did Casey have a family?" I asked.

He smeared a hand over his hair. "Yeah, and that's sad, too. He was keeping a crippled daughter who'll end up in an institution now because there isn't anybody else to take care of her. Jesus, when you think of the amount of misery some trigger-happy moron can cause, you figure maybe it's time for the big bomb and a whole new start."

"But would it be any better the second time around?"

"Probably not," he conceded morosely.

I took the elevator down and went back to where I'd left the car. It was twenty to three. Gratefully I realized I'd probably have time for one quiet drink. I drove out to Englewood, found a small bar, ordered a double Scotch and took it over to a table to avoid bartender small talk. I wanted to brood. I drank the Scotch very slowly and brooded, giving myself exactly half an hour. When I came out of the place I noticed a drive-in across the street and decided a few ham sandwiches and Cokes might come in handy. While I was waiting for them I got some change and went into the public phone booth. I called the office first.

"Rutledge and Kramer," Mickey said brightly.

"This is Kramer. Thought I'd better check in with you and see if there's anything new on the home front."

"There sure is. Guess what."

"Tell me."

"He's just back from court and in there puffing his pipe a mile a minute. So that crisis is over."

"Happy day," I said. "Call Doris."

"I already have. Is there any use in asking you where you are and what you're doing?"

"Having a crisis of my own, I think. But if all goes well I'll see you in the morning."

"And if all doesn't go well?"

"Be prepared to bail me out of the clink."

Or even the morgue, I thought as I hung up. I laid out some more change for the toll call and asked the operator to get me the sheriff's office up at West Bend. Having deposited thirty-five cents I got a voice that informed me the sheriff was not in.

"Who is this?" I asked.

"Deputy Gilbert."

"All right, I've got a message for you, listen carefully. You know the Castle property over near Piñon Point? Place where a doctor died in a fire about three years ago?"

"Yeah, what about it?"

"There's a body buried back in the woods there," I said. "I discovered it when I was hunting up there this afternoon. Find the stream that runs down back of the cabin site and follow it to where I left a scarf tied to a branch. Then hit up the slope to where I tied a handkerchief to a stick stuck in the ground. Got it?"

"Who is this?" he shouted.

Time to hang up. I hung up, and went back to the car. The carhop was on her way with my sack of ham sandwiches and Cokes. I paid her and tipped her.

Then I headed down to Yuba.

17

Not one of the garden spots of the world, Yuba—just a wide unpaved main street guarded by drooping cottonwoods, and a couple of blocks of old weatherbeaten business buildings. Rainier was already there, parked in front of a feed store a little down from the bar and grocery, where a handful of other cars were clustered. Neither of us signaled as I drifted past very slowly, allowing him time to get started and pull out. In a minute he had passed me and bore left out of town away from the main highway. It was a good country road, cutting straight as a string through flat farming and grazing country. Two cars whizzed by in a cloud of dust during the five-, six-mile run before he signaled for a right turn at a cross roads. That put us on a one-lane dirt road that looked as if it served a single farm or ranch. I wondered what you did if you met a car coming out, but fortunately that didn't happen. In a few minutes we hit a wooded area. Rainier slowed, watching for something along the left side of the road now. That proved to be a platform of planks bridging the roadside ditch. We crossed it and followed a faint trail that wound back in among the trees and ended in a clearing where heaps of sawdust and stacks of cordwood testified to the reason for the trail.

Rainier turned around in the clearing, stopped and cut his engine. I did the same and we both got out.

"This is the best cover possible," he said. "And it's so late in the day nobody's apt to be coming in here to cut or haul wood. The bridge was about a mile ahead on that first road. So we're about a mile east of the stream bed and maybe two miles upstream from the bridge. We'll have to cut across a stretch of open field to get over to the stream bed, but after that there's pretty good cover."

I gave him an appraising glance. He was uptight, his face grim and set. I couldn't blame him, of course. He had a lot riding on what we were about to do.

"I'll get the stuff I brought," he said.

He took a large flashlight and a thick coil of clothesline from the back of his car.

"What about the gun?" I asked.

He patted his midriff.

"I'll take it," I said.

His face hardened. Not an easy man to deal with, Mr. Leslie Rainier. "Like hell you will," he snapped.

"Listen, Rainier," I said evenly. "You're mad and you're hating. That and a gun is the kind of a combination that can get you into a worse mess, instead of getting you out of the one you're in. I'll take it."

For a moment he glowered uncompromisingly. Then with a shrug he succumbed, jerked his jacket open, pulled a small automatic pistol from the waistband of his trousers.

"It's a Colt thirty-two six-shot, fully loaded," he said sarcastically. "Try not to blow your foot off."

I let him have the crack to help with his sore feelings and tucked the gun into my jacket pocket.

"I brought some sandwiches and Coke," I said, and turned to my car to get them. As I straightened up from leaning in the open window I heard him behind me, had a second of warning before the heavy flashlight connected with my skull—a second of warning that allowed me to duck just enough to escape the worst of the blow. It stunned me, but I managed to whirl in a crouch and come up with an uppercut to his chin. His head snapped back and he reeled away and I bore in fast, driving both fists into his midriff while he was still off balance. He doubled over and I landed another uppercut that sent him sprawling. He rolled away and tried to scramble to his feet. I threw myself on him, bore him down again and wrenched the flashlight out of his flailing arm and tossed it. I had him face down in the dirt now, my hands clamped on his neck, my legs locked around his middle.

"One more move and I'll put you to sleep for a week," I panted.

He'd had enough of it and offered no resistance while I wrenched off my necktie, jerked his arms back and bound them together at the wrists. Then I got up and he rolled onto his back and sat up.

"Of all the stupid stunts to pull!" I snapped. "Why?"
He glared at me in stubborn sullen silence.
"All right, get up," I ordered.

He scrambled awkwardly to his feet. I picked up the flashlight and the coil of clothesline, retrieved the sack of sandwiches and Cokes.

"We've still got a job to do. You lead the way and don't try to pull anything, because you're no good to me now anyway and I could just as well leave you by the wayside. Understand?"

He stood panting a little, his chin on his chest, his face a mask of repressed fury.

"Get going!" I said coldly.

He turned and stalked off into the woods beyond the clearing. Ten minutes of fast walking and we were out of the trees. Ahead was open field. We struck out across it as rapidly as possible. This was the worst stretch, no cover at all. It was a relief to reach the shelter of heavy brush, alders and cottonwood saplings on the bank of the stream bed. We descended into it. It was bone dry, a rocky gulch worn deep by centuries of rushing floodwaters. About wide enough for the two of us to walk abreast, but I kept back a ways, taking no chances with him. We continued to move cautiously, crouching down when we weren't sheltered by brush along the banks. Fifteen minutes of slipping and scrambling over rocks and we reached the bridge. It was a rough wooden affair on top of two stone retaining walls. We scrambled in under it.

"Sit down with your back close to the wall," I ordered Rainier.

He obeyed, huddling down with his chin sunk on his chest and his eyes closed, breathing hard from the walk. I unloaded the stuff I'd carried and flopped down myself. Rainier raised his head finally.

"Untie me," he said. "It was a stupid thing to do and I promise you I won't make any more trouble."

"I'm afraid I don't trust you, Mr. Rainier," I said.

"Why not? I just—lost my head for a minute. I was mad because you took the gun."

"Sure. And what were you going to do with the gun? Kill

whoever comes here—and me too? Did you think you could get away with that?"

"No. But I couldn't trust you, and I wanted you out of commission long enough to—to do what Mavis and I have to do."

"What's that?"

"Get out of the country. Listen, I'm leveling with you, Kramer. I've hired a pilot friend to fly us down to Mexico in a chartered plane late tonight."

"After you'd killed these characters we're expecting."

"No," he protested. "I was going to capture them and turn them over to the police. But I knew everything would bust open then. Including the possibility that Castle is alive. And if he is, you know as well as I do what will happen. Mavis will be charged with collusion. I'm not going to let her stay here and go through that. And I was afraid you'd try to stop us from clearing out."

I opened the paper sack and fished out a can of Coke and opened it and took a long swallow. "If Mavis is innocent she can be cleared of collusion charges," I said.

"Don't give me that. Who'd believe her? Who'd—"

He broke off as we both heard a car in the distance. It came on rapidly and hit the bridge, rattling the wooden flooring deafeningly, sending down a shower of dust and dirt. Slowly the sound diminished and faded away.

"I take it this is only a service road for a few ranches or farms," I said.

He nodded. "I've checked it out often enough. For the most part there isn't a car in hours."

"You've wanted to do this before," I said.

"Yes. Mavis always stopped me. But this time even she couldn't do that."

"Does Mavis know she's flying to Mexico tonight?"

"Not yet."

"You think she'll do it?"

"If she loves me, yes. If she wants to save her own skin, yes."

"Suppose we learn that Dr. Castle is not alive," I said.

"That would be different. We wouldn't have to go. But I think he is alive."

"What would you use for money in Mexico?"

"Mavis got that fifty thousand from the banks this morning. You told her not to, just to stuff the briefcase with paper. We did that. But I told her to pick up the money anyway."

"On what pretext?"

"That we didn't know what might happen here, and if we flubbed it we might still need the money." He paused. "And I've got a wad of cash stashed in my apartment. We'd make out."

I put down my Coke and scrambled over to where he sat and motioned him to twist around a little. I'd tied him very tight, but the knot finally yielded. He groaned with relief as he brought his hands around and fell to chafing his wrists.

"Do anything I don't like," I said, "and I'll put a bullet through your leg."

He nodded heavily. Then he said, "Does this mean you think Dr. Castle is not alive?"

"No. It means I think you wouldn't have told me all this if you really intended to do it."

He didn't say anything to that. I got another Coke and handed it over and he drank deeply, but shook his head to the offer of a sandwich. I didn't feel particularly hungry myself, but at six-thirty I ate one of them anyway, more to pass time than anything else. The sun was dropping behind distant hills now, and it was growing cooler. I wished I'd thought to pack a heavier jacket and regretted not having brought cigarettes. Knowing it would be safer not to smoke, I'd left them in the car, and Rainier didn't smoke. Time dragged. Another car, jeep from the sound of it, thundered over us about seven.

"Which way does Mavis throw the briefcase?" I asked.

"To the left, from the driver's side of the car. She's not supposed to get out of it at all, just lower the window and toss it."

"Good. Then we'll know exactly where to be waiting."

I could feel myself tensing up as the minutes inched on, the way you do when what's going to happen is mostly unknown and you're going to have to play a dangerous situation by ear. Rainier looked at his watch every five minutes. His nerves were giving me nerves. And the cramped position we had to maintain up close to the retaining wall didn't help.

"Ten to eight," he muttered finally. "It shouldn't be long now."

It wasn't. Almost on the dot of eight we heard the car approaching slowly. It rumbled onto the bridge and stopped. There were a few small sounds and then the briefcase came spinning down to the left, landed with a solid thwack. The car motor roared and the car surged away in a burst of speed.

"Will she come back this way?" I asked.

"Yes, she turns around at the next access road and goes back through Yuba. That's an order, too, and probably means she's watched in Yuba. Timed too, I expect—to make sure she doesn't try to pull anything." It was growing quite dark under the bridge and he had to angle his wrist to get a little daylight on his watch. "Timing it now—eight minutes or so for her to get back to Yuba, the same for them to get out here, if they merely wait to make sure she has returned."

Her car was coming back now, moving much faster. It thundered over the bridge and went on. The briefcase had landed in the middle of the gulch, well beyond the bridge opening. I wriggled over to where I could see the two banks. The one to the left was by far the easiest to come down, probably the one that would be used. I dropped to my hands and knees and crawled out, got the briefcase and planted it in close to the left retaining wall.

"If it's the girl," I said, "we'll be in luck. I'll try to grab her before she can make an outcry, and gamble that whoever may be with her will come down here to see what's wrong."

"And if he doesn't?"

"Well, we couldn't possibly rush the car before he could get away. So we just gamble and hope."

I gave it ten minutes, then I said, "I think we should get in position now. They may stop the car at a distance and somebody make the approach on foot, in which case we won't hear anything until the last moment. Here—" I handed him the flashlight. "Try not to use it on me, but it's a weapon if you need it."

We stood up and stationed ourselves along the left-side retaining wall. I was closer to the opening, Rainier right behind me. Dusk was settling down fast now. A wind had come up, rustling leaves in the brush along the bank. Fifteen, perhaps twenty more minutes passed; I could no longer see my watch. Then I heard the car coming. It came on fast, clattered over the bridge, went straight on. The sound of it seemed to die away for a moment, then began again very faintly and far away. The same car coming back, I decided. It moved slowly now, rumbled over the bridge—and stopped. Silence. Then the click of a door opening. I strained back against the wall, every muscle tensed.

The next thing I heard was the sudden rush and rattle of stones and the crackling of brush, followed by a muted curse, as somebody came sliding down the left embankment. I reached into my pocket for the gun and butt-ended it in my hand. Then a large dark form loomed in the opening—no woman this. He spotted the briefcase and bent to grab it and he was no more than a yard from where I stood.

I landed on his back and brought the butt end of the gun down on his skull. He folded with a long soft "Whoof." I dragged him in under the bridge and dropped him. Then I moved out from the shelter of the bridge a little ways and scrambled around, crouching and beating the brush clumsily. Several minutes passed. Finally a car door clicked again.

"What's the matter?" It was a woman's voice—hoarse, alarmed.

"Can't find the damned thing," I growled, neutralizing my voice as much as possible. "Give me a hand."

She came sliding down the bank and I spun around and grabbed her. She screamed.

"Skip it," I said. "We've got your friend." There was just enough light for me to see her face—or rather her hair. And she wasn't a total surprise.

Viola.

"Drag him out here where we can see a little better," I called to Rainier. "And bring the rope and flashlight."

"You hit him pretty hard," he panted, hauling the limp body into the open. He turned it over and beamed the flashlight onto a bearded face.

"Daddy Baker," I said. "Well, what do you know about that?"

Rainier was leaning over him. He stared up at me. "*Who?*"

"A hippie running a commune down south of Astoria. His real name is Conrad Baker, but the hippies call him Daddy."

Rainier rose slowly and said, "You're wrong, Kramer. This man is Ted Wood."

18

IT SHOOK me enough so that I momentarily loosened my grip on Viola. She wrenched away and scrambled for the bank. I lunged and hauled her back and pulled the necktie I'd used on Rainier from my pocket and tied her wrists behind her back. Then I shoved her toward a large stone.

"You may as well sit and be comfortable, sister, because you sure as hell aren't going anywhere. Now, what about it? Is this guy Ted Wood?"

She had retreated into her hair and refused to answer.

I knelt beside the inert body on the ground. "You're sure?" I said to Rainier.

"I'm sure. He's fifty pounds heavier and looks quite different with this shaven head and beard. But it's him all right."

He was breathing heavily, but breathing. Concussion, maybe. I searched him swiftly. No gun. A wallet fat with bills and all the necessary cards to prove he was Conrad Baker. Nothing difficult about getting these if you knew the right people. And finally from his inside jacket pocket I pulled an airline ticket envelope.

As of ten-forty tonight Mr. C. Baker was flying to Mexico City. One-way trip.

I got to my feet. "He knew it was getting too hot. One more haul—and out. All right, start tying him up. Wrists and ankles. Tie good. And you—" I swung around to Viola—"start talking."

No answer. She was like a little rabbit in that hutch of hair. I went over and pulled some of it back and wadded it down into the collar of her jacket so I could see her face. It was scared, but defiant.

"I've got nothing to say," she snarled. "I don't even know what this is all about."

I picked up the briefcase. "You didn't know there was fifty thousand bucks in this? You didn't know why you came out here on a lonely country road to get it? You didn't know your friend here was your old bedmate, Ted Wood? You're just an innocent bystander? Then let me straighten you out. You and Ted Wood have been extorting money from Mavis Castle for two years. You're the gal who does the phoning because Mavis Castle might recognize his voice if he tried to do it. So how much of a cut do you get, Viola? Come on —talk."

"Why should I? You can't prove a thing."

"Don't kid yourself we can't. Mavis Castle will identify your voice. And Ted Wood will sing once he wakes up. He'll sing loud and long, because this isn't only extortion, baby—it's murder. With him and you in it right up to your necks."

"Murder!" she shrilled. "You're crazy. Nobody was killed. That doc died in the fire, just the way it looked."

"If it was all that simple, why did Ted Wood change his

identity? Why did the two of you kill that private detective who came looking for him?"

"We didn't. You don't even know that guy is dead. Sure, you came along and said he was. But you were snowing me. It's never been in the papers."

"It will be by morning. Along with who killed him, and that's you and Ted Wood. If Manning had caught on to your little extortion racket you could have paid him off. But with murder it was different. You couldn't take a chance on him keeping still about that, not at any price. So you had to kill him."

She lurched to her feet, stared at me wild-eyed in the beam of the flashlight.

"If he was killed, I had nothing to do with it. All I ever did was make those calls for Ted. This is the first time I even came along on a pickup. And I had to, because he was leaving for Mexico City tonight and I needed my take. I needed it bad."

She was falling apart fast, and I bore in fast. "So he was clearing out and leaving you to take the rap."

"We figured nobody could tie me in. And he was giving me an extra thousand."

"You figured wrong. Now I want the truth. Did he kill Dr. Castle?"

"No—no, I swear it. I'll tell you how it was. He read in the paper how that doc died in the fire, see? And he had done a lot of snooping while he worked for them. He knew the widow would be collecting all that bread, the insurance money. So he said—he said he had an idea."

"Like?"

"He didn't tell me what it was. He said he had to do some investigating first. Then he split, just like I told you before. I don't know where he went or what he was doing, and that's the God's truth. He was gone almost a year. Then he came back and got in touch with me."

"Calling himself Conrad Baker by then?"

"Yes."

"Was he down in Astoria?"

"No, he was in Denver."

"All right, what did he tell you?"

"He told me nothing. He just offered me a deal. I was to call Mrs. Castle and tell her I knew her husband was alive. Name the price for silence and arrange the pickup. I got five thousand every time."

"You're sure he didn't tell you where he'd been or what he'd been doing after he split."

"He said he'd been laying low, that's all."

"Did he say Dr. Castle really was alive?"

"No. But what did that matter, so long as we could make the widow think he might be?"

Rainier had done a fast and efficient job of securing Ted Wood, and except for a few groans as he was rolled around Wood hadn't come to. Now Rainier was standing at my side, staring at the girl.

"You just coldbloodedly put her through all that hell?" he demanded bitterly.

"I wasn't running the show," she said sullenly. "I only did what I was told to do."

I caught Rainier's arm. "Take it easy. Don't blow it now. Listen, Viola, I'm going to ask you again. Do you think Ted killed Dr. Castle and arranged to make it look like an accident?"

"No!" she fairly shouted. "I already told you no. Ted never killed him. Why would he?"

"There could have been several reasons. One, he was sore at him for firing him for a theft he hadn't really committed. Two, he could have done it just to set up an extortion situation. He'd snooped and knew all about that insurance policy with the double indemnity for accidental death. He knew the widow would collect a lot of money. He knew a badly burned body couldn't be identified beyond a shadow of a doubt. And knowing that much, he could see the possibilities."

"I don't care what he knew," she cried. "Ted never killed anyone."

"How can you be so sure? You've already admitted he was still living with you when the story about Dr. Castle came out in the papers. Right after that he split. Why—unless he had had something to do with that so-called accidental death?"

"I don't know why," she yelled. "Ask him—if you haven't killed him."

"How did that private detective catch on to the fact that Daddy Baker was really Ted Wood?"

"Who says he did? I told you I told that dick nothing—nothing but what I told you that first time we rapped. He couldn't have found Ted."

"Why not? He was casing all the hippie areas and he had a picture of Ted Wood. I say he could have gone up to Cricket Town just like I did and recognized Daddy Baker for Ted Wood. What's more, he knew about the Castle affair and Ted's connection with the Castles, because he came to Mrs. Castle and asked questions about Ted."

"Then maybe you'd better ask *her* what happened to that guy. Who had more reason than she had to want to keep everything hushed up? She believed her husband was alive and knew damned well that she as well as he could be clobbered with an insurance swindle rap if the truth came out."

Rainier lunged for her. I grabbed him and hauled him back. "Don't be a fool. We've got this sewed up and ready for the police. If she's lying or concealing anything they'll find it out. Let's get a move on now."

"What are we going to do with him?"

"I think it's better we don't move him. He'll be safe enough here even if he comes to. You take the girl in to the Englewood police and have them send an ambulance out. Tell them you've made a citizen's arrest and are charging her with extortion. Have them also get in touch with the sheriff up at West Bend. They should have the body out by now."

"And you?"

"I've got another little piece of business to take care of. I'll keep your gun, if you don't mind. Come on, let's go."

I herded Viola up the bank ahead of us. Their car, a black Volvo, was standing at the edge of the road just beyond the bridge. We got in, Viola between us, and me driving. She was sulky and resigned by now. I headed back to where we'd left our own cars, and we transferred her to Rainier's car.

"Ride nice with the nice man, now," I said. "He doesn't like you and I hate to think of what he might do if you try to give him trouble."

Her hair had slipped back over her face and she was probably glaring at me from behind it, but what I couldn't see wouldn't hurt me.

"Step on it," I said to Rainier.

I made a quick search of the Volvo after he had pulled

out of the woods. There was nothing in it but the luggage Ted Wood had been taking along to Mexico City, three large heavy bags. I decided not to waste time going through them. I left the keys in the ignition and climbed into my own car.

19

I ROLLED into Astoria at ten-fifteen and went straight over to the High Tor. There was a light on in her room and she opened the door on the chain when I knocked.

"You! What on earth, Phil?"

"Better late than never. Or were you expecting someone else?"

"No—no, of course not. But I'm still not feeling well. Whatever it is, since it's so late could we leave it until morning?"

"No, we couldn't," I said. "Better let me in, Holly."

Reluctantly she snapped the chain off and allowed me to enter. Far from being in dishabille, she was fully dressed, looking very lovely indeed, and two packed bags were standing by the door. A light coat and her purse were lying on the bed. She had a cigarette in her hand.

"Your cold seems to be much better," I said. "And it would appear you are going somewhere."

"Yes, I'm leaving." She turned away nervously. "I—I've decided to drop the whole thing and I have a reservation for an early-morning flight out of Denver, so I thought I'd drive up there for tonight. I intended to call you in the morning and tell you to just forget everything."

"That's interesting. The picture certainly changed in a hurry, didn't it?"

"I—I guess it is a little sudden." She went to the dressing table, stabbed the cigarette out in a tray. "But I don't like what we've gotten into. Ted is either dead or in trouble—serious trouble. Either way, what's the use of going on with this? We're only stirring up things that—are none of our business."

"But I've found Ted," I said.

She froze where she stood. "You've—*what?*"

"I've found Ted, Holly. Or should I say Virginia?" I walked over to her. "You look surprised. But no more surprised than I was when I tumbled. You are really Virginia Logan and you aren't Ted Wood's sister and never were. And Ted Wood is in custody along with Viola. Leslie Rainier and I captured them tonight when they attempted to pick up the fifty thousand. So, you see, Ted won't be coming with the money, which is what you were waiting here for, right?"

She backed slowly to the bed and sank down in it. Her face was a study in mixed emotions—dismay, anger, fear.

"As a matter of fact," I continued, "Ted had a plane ticket for Mexico City on him and would have been airborne just about now if he hadn't come a cropper. So I'd be willing to bet my last stiver he never intended to rush down here and share the fifty thou with you before he took off. It was pretty foolish of you to believe he would."

"That—that dirty rotten—" she began slowly and thickly.

"Tut, tut. Bad words will redress no wrongs. Instead of wasting time on that, let's have a few explanations."

She turned and reached for the big white purse. I moved very fast and got there just as her pretty paw dipped in.

"Drop it," I said, tightening my hand on her wrist.

She squealed and dropped it. "I—I only wanted a cigarette."

I stepped back with the purse. The gun was a small six-shot .25 automatic, the kind that might not stop a man with one slug, but surely would if the slugs kept coming. I dropped it into my pocket and extracted the airline ticket. As of eight-thirty tomorrow morning Miss V. Logan was departing for New York City from Denver's Stapleton. I threw it down on the dressing table, placed the bag beside it.

"What bugs me," I said bitterly, "is how you could have been stupid enough to think you could pressure him into handing over that money or even part of it."

"It was worth a try, wasn't it?" She huddled on the edge of the bed, nursing her sore wrist. "How did you find out he was Ted?"

"Rainier recognized him even with the extra weight and the beard. And Viola sang, of course. After that I knew you must have recognized him when we went up to Cricket Town. I'll give you both credit; you carried it off beautifully, considering it must have been a nasty shock to him and a first-class stroke of luck for you. Or so you thought. When did you contact him?"

"The next morning."

"And demanded fifty thousand?"

"Yes."

"Or you'd spill everything?"

"Yes. He said he didn't have it, would have to make another pitch to Mavis Castle. And the best he'd give me was a fifty-fifty split." She straightened, brought her chin

up defiantly. "Okay, so I didn't get it. In view of everything else, that's just as well. It leaves me clean."

"Not quite. It was still attempted extortion."

"What do you mean?" she cried indignantly. "I didn't
have a thing to do with *that*."

"You triggered it with your demands."

"So what? Sooner or later he'd have made another pitch
on his own, anyway."

"You were also planning on half the proceeds."

"Nobody knows that but you."

"He knows it. You think he won't talk?"

"Why should he? Throwing me to the wolves won't be a
bit of help to him. No, I don't think he'll talk. And if you'll
keep still I don't have to get mixed up in this at all. I've
paid you well and I'll pay you more—just name your price.
But for God's sake give me a break."

"I can't. I don't know the rest of it. I don't know where
else you fit in—or how you fit at all."

"I'll tell you," she cried eagerly. "I'll tell you everything
if you'll let me off the hook."

"That depends on what the story is," I said. "And
whether I think you're telling the truth."

"Okay, okay. Can I have a cigarette?"

I lit one, handed it to her, lit another for myself and
pulled a chair around. "Talk," I said.

"Well, to start with, when I went home to Michigan,
David and I were already washed up. I knew I'd never see
him again and didn't much care. In fact, I didn't even know
he was dead until Ted showed up there in Arlington."

"And when was that?"

"Several weeks after David died."

"Was he calling himself Conrad Baker then?"

"No, but he wasn't calling himself Ted Wood either. He

was using another name. He had changed over the minute he dumped Viola and left Astoria."

"Why?"

"He knew there'd be a big investigation of that fire and a disgruntled ex-employee would be in for a severe grilling. As a hippie, he'd be even more suspect. And he just didn't want to take any chances on it. He felt they could hang something on him even though he hadn't had a thing to do with it. That may sound like he had something to hide. But it's hippie psychology to fear the fuzz. You know they take plenty of undeserved persecution."

"All right, I'll buy that. Tell me how Ted knew where you were. Obviously he knew about your affair with Dr. Castle."

"Yes, of course he did. A couple of times while he was still working there David had taken me to the house, while Mavis was gone. So Ted knew who I was, and he knew where I worked. It was easy enough for him to make an inquiry there and find out where I'd gone."

"So what did he want of you?"

"He believed that David and I had pulled an insurance swindle, and he wanted half of what he assumed we were going to get out of Mavis."

"And had you pulled an insurance swindle?"

She gestured impatiently. "Don't be an idiot. We had not. David died accidentally in that fire. That's all there was to it. Oh, Ted wouldn't believe it, either, at first. He gave me a rough time. But I finally convinced him. It was then that he came up with another idea. He pointed out that maybe Mavis could be made to believe that David was still alive. And on the strength of that he and I could con her out of some of that insurance money."

I looked at her intently. "You're sure that was *his* idea?"

"Yes."

"I don't see why he'd count you in. He could have pulled it himself, couldn't he? You're sure it wasn't your idea?"

"If it had been, couldn't I have pulled it by myself?"

"Maybe you didn't want to risk your own pretty neck, preferred to let him take the chances."

"No, it was a little more complicated than that." She paused, flicked ashes into the tray on the bedside stand, then said defensively, "Look. I was stuck in this little town, my mother dying, the future pretty uncertain. I was lonely, I needed someone. And he was attractive and willing. Maybe we weren't in love, but so what? We had a good thing going."

"You were also under police surveillance. Weren't they curious about this boy friend of yours?"

"They may have been. But he was using another name and he had picked up a job in a local store. He looked legit enough. Besides, the one thing they were watching for was evidence that David was alive and that I was in contact with him."

"True. So what then?"

"My mother died, I settled things up and in June I took off for Cleveland. I had a friend there, knew I could get a job. And Ted went back to Denver. The idea was that we should part ways until he could make sure the widow had received the insurance money." She scrubbed the cigarette out in the tray and looked at me bitterly. "So maybe you know what happened then."

"I can guess by the look on your face."

She nodded. "Exactly. I never heard from him again. I stayed in Cleveland for six months, hoping in that stupid way you do. Then I went on to New York. I kept telling myself it was just as well, that the plan had been too dangerous anyway, that he'd end up dead or in the pen and it would serve him right. But I also kept thinking about the way he'd double-crossed me. It got to rankling more and more. I had banked ten thousand from the sale of my mother's house. And finally I decided to gamble it on an effort to find Ted."

"And pry some of that nice black bread out of him."

"Why not? I sent Manning first."

"And Manning found him. And Ted made sure he'd never get back to you with the information."

She shook her head slowly. "I don't think so. He claims he didn't kill Manning, and I'm inclined to believe him. I think Manning would have had a price and Ted would have paid it."

"I could buy that, except that I'm sure it's Manning up there in that grave. And if it is, who had a better motive than Ted?"

"Mavis and Rainier. Maybe just Mavis, for that matter. Because . . ."

"Because what?"

"Because maybe David *is* alive, after all. He wasn't the kind of a guy who'd count me in. But that doesn't mean he wasn't the kind of a guy who could have pulled a swindle like that and gotten Mavis to go along, too. Even Rainier wouldn't have had to know."

I got up and walked over to the window. I thought of the little repair-shop man sprawled dead in front of his safe. Maybe for nothing more than a three-year-old slip of paper —a slip of paper that had been the crux of the matter the whole time.

"Phil—"

She was at my side. I looked at her. She'd taken me for a big fat ride, and it was hurting. It was hurting because she still looked very beautiful and desirable. The truly evil repel you, but she wasn't that evil. Just human and weak with the age-old itch for the fast easy buck if an occasion seemed to present itself. You could deplore it. But you couldn't break out with moral measles over it.

"Phil, I've told the truth," she said huskily. "Every word of it is true, so help me. All it amounts to is that I had some bad intentions, only I never got to first base with any of them. What's to hold me for? I can't even give evidence that others can't give just as well. Let me go."

She reached for my hand. I evaded her touch and swung away.

"All right," I said. "You've sold me. I'm leaving now and I was never here." I went to the door. "Do what you please."

"Wait—"

"What is it?"

"I'm grateful. Couldn't we part—like friends?"

"No," I said. "We couldn't quite do that."

"At least let me tell you I'm sorry for the lies, for the way I deceived you."

I shrugged. "Forget it. I've got a talent for picking 'em wrong."

Outside I stood and looked up at the sky for a moment. It was vast and empty and lonely. So was I. But I didn't have time to indulge my feelings. I climbed into the car and headed back to Denver.

20

THERE WERE lights upstairs when I rolled up the drive at
the side of the house. It was twelve-thirty, the neighborhood
mostly dark and silent. I stopped the car, cut the lights and
ignition, got out, slamming the door. That woke a dog; it
began to howl from somewhere down the street as I punched
the doorbell—a long steady ring.

It was several minutes before a light flashed on downstairs. Then I heard steps behind the door. "Who is it?"

"Phil Kramer. I'm sorry to bother you at such an hour,
Miss Parker, but it's very important that I see you."

The key turned in the lock and she stood there, clutching
the robe around her.

"This *is* an imposition," she said angrily. "What on earth
do you want?"

"May I come in?"

"At this hour of the night, no, you may not."

"Look, Miss Parker," I said wearily, "I'm no happier
about the hour of the night than you are. But—"

"Oh, all right, all right," she grumbled. "You're here, so
come in."

She opened the screen door and stepped back to let me walk on into the living room. A single lamp was burning; the room looked cold and gloomy. Uninvited I took a chair. She stood and regarded me with disapproval.

"You look a mess, I must say."

That I probably did—tieless, dusty, rumpled, maybe a few bruises blooming.

"It's been a rough evening, Miss Parker. In fact, so much has happened that I was sure you'd want to hear about it."

"I think," she said acidly, "I could have controlled my impatience until morning. However, since you're here, what has happened?"

"First," I said, "the body of Ben Manning, the private detective, has been found."

It didn't jolt her; she merely raised an eyebrow. "It has? That's interesting. Where?"

"Buried up on the Castle property near the site of the cabin. He had been shot. Slugs from his body were sent down here early this evening for ballistic study and I've just talked to a Lieutenant Foster at Homicide who says they match slugs taken from the body of a man shot around eight, nine o'clock this morning—or would that be yesterday morning? No matter, the man I'm speaking of ran a type-writer repair shop about seven blocks from where you work, Miss Parker."

She regarded me impassively. "Well?"

"Your cold seems better. I assume you went to work to-day."

"Of course I went to work."

"At what time did you get there?"

"Eight o'clock, as usual."

"Others could verify that?"

"Certainly. I talked to several co-workers when I came in."

"You could prove exactly where you were between eight and nine?"

"I could. I was in my office dictating some routine letters for Dr. Braddock's secretary to type up."

"The secretary was present?"

"No. I was using a dictaphone. But what of it? His secretary can tell you I brought the work out to her at a little after nine."

"Work that could have been done at some other time. I'm afraid that's not a very good alibi, Miss Parker."

"Alibi!" She pulled herself up ramrod straight. "Are you implying that I need an alibi, Mr. Kramer?"

I shook my head slowly. "On the contrary, I'm telling you it wouldn't do you any good to have one, Miss Parker. The fact that Casey and Ben Manning were shot with the same gun is conclusive evidence that these two murders tie in. And there is no one but you with a real motive for killing them."

She backed to the fireplace and regarded me with naked astonishment. "You're accusing me of—of murdering these two men?"

"I'm accusing you of murdering three men, Miss Parker. For obviously you would have had no reason to kill Casey and Manning unless you had killed Dr. Castle too."

"You're out of your mind," she gasped.

"Am I? Listen. You remember Rufus Langley's story about his typewriter? How Dr. Castle told the nurse who called from the Four Pines that it wouldn't be ready until Saturday? How you, when I mentioned this, assured me that Dr. Castle probably already had the typewriter and was just stalling to avoid having to take it down to Rufus right away? That was convincing enough, Miss Parker— perfectly possible and all that. Except that Casey was killed so someone could get hold of a customer's slip that would prove the typewriter *was* picked up on Saturday?"

"How could you possibly know that?"

"Because he was killed with the same gun that killed Ben Manning. Otherwise, yes, it might have passed for a bur- glary attempt that blew up and ended in murder. So let's spell it out, Miss Parker. Somebody did pick up that type- writer Saturday afternoon. We can be reasonably sure that Dr. Castle did not interrupt his weekend drunk to drive all the way down here for it. So I think it's much more likely that before he left the office Friday noon he told you to pick it up."

Silence.

"Which I'm sure you did do, Miss Parker," I went on. "And then took it up to Dr. Castle Saturday night."

She stared at me stonily. "Are you completely out of your mind? Why on earth would I have taken it up there?"

"As an excuse to see him."

"*See* him! I saw him practically every day of my life."

"Yes, in the impersonal atmosphere of the office. But you wanted to see him where you could be alone with him, where you could tell him how you still felt, perhaps plead with him to take you back. In other words, you were still in love with him, Miss Parker. Your affair with him was long over, yes —but you hadn't stopped caring, far from it. And you hadn't stopped hoping and dreaming that you could make him care again."

She threw her head back and laughed. "You are very funny, Mr. Kramer—I mean, crudely comic, of course."

"Am I? Then why is Ben Manning dead?"

"A sleazy little man like that? Why, I would say there are dozens of reasons why he could be dead."

"Why do you describe him as a sleazy little man, Miss Parker? Apparently that's exactly what he was. But you told me he had never come to see you."

She gestured sharply. "Aren't all private detectives sleazy little men?"

"Not at all. And since Ben Manning saw everyone else who was even remotely connected with this affair I find it impossible to believe that he missed you."

Without warning, anger flared in her eyes. Her face reddened and the cords of her neck tightened. "I'm sick of what you believe or don't believe, Mr. Kramer. I am sick of your stupid deductions and assumptions. I've taken enough. Get out of here."

"Not until I've said it plainly, Miss Parker. No deduction, no assumption, but a plain fact. You killed Dr. Castle. He spurned you again that Saturday night and it was the last straw and you killed him. Oh, you got away with it, you managed to make it look like an accident. But when Ben Manning came here you saw at once that if he started poking into the affair he might break it wide open—a second time around, the truth could be uncovered. You sized him up correctly for a sleazy little private detective who, if he simply disappeared, could be assumed to have been killed in some alley or back room for any one of a dozen sleazy reasons. So you killed him on the spot. As you probably would have killed me when I first came here if I had been alone. But there were two of us, one too many for you to hope to handle."

"You're alone tonight, Mr. Kramer," she said, and took

her hand from her pocket. Gripped firmly in her fist was a small snub-nosed pistol.

"So I was right," I said.

She stared at me, her eyes as cold as the one cold eye of the gun. "Yes. I did go up there that Saturday night, using the typewriter as an excuse, pretending I thought he would want it. David was drinking as usual. I—I told him how I felt, that I couldn't live without him. I begged him, on my knees I begged him to—to be kind to me—"

She broke off for a moment. When she resumed, her voice had changed, gone slack, dry and empty. "But you can't do it that way, can you? You can't get love by begging for it, by wanting it so desperately that you'd crawl for it. He . . . he only said awful things to me—cruel hateful things. He laughed at me, he said I was ridiculous. He told me to get out. Finally I left and drove partway down the lane toward the main road. Then I stopped and—and just sat there. I don't know for how long—an hour maybe, maybe longer. And everything was turning to hatred inside me."

She stopped again. "You don't understand that, do you? Or do you?" Her eyes went over my face, slowly, wonderingly, as if searching for an answer. "Do you know how cruel desire can be, when it's utterly hopeless? There was a poet who knew. He said that desire was bronze-clawed, like a hawk. He was right—oh, he was so right. That's what it is: a pair of claws that fasten on your heart and flesh— that rip and tear at you until every decent feeling you ever had is slashed to shreds. Until finally there's nothing left but the hatred—the pain and the hatred. Can you understand that?"

I nodded. "I think I understand, Miss Parker. He had caused you extreme anguish. You wanted him to suffer as you had suffered."

"Yes, there at the end, yes. That was all that was left—
to make him suffer, too. I got out of the car and walked back
to the cabin. He was dead drunk by then—sprawled on the
bed in the bedroom, snoring. I got shavings and kindling
from the woodpile, some bedding and clothes, and strewed
them around the room. Then I poured gasoline on everything. One match was all I had to toss—there was barely
time for me to get out. I had the key to the door, I locked it
behind me. I picked up a stone and broke a cellar window
and threw the key into the cellar. Then I ran . . . and
ran . . ."

She paused, and something quivered in her stony face
for a moment, as if the memory had caught at some still-
vulnerable chord of feeling. But then her expression hardened again. "I'm not sorry. I've never been sorry. My only
regret is that he probably didn't suffer much, that he may
have been asphyxiated by smoke without ever realizing
what was happening. I'd like to think that he did wake up
and tried to get out of there, that he had a few minutes of
knowing he was trapped in that inferno." She broke off
again. "But you wouldn't understand *that*, would you?"

I sighed. "I don't think I've ever hated anyone quite that
much, Miss Parker. Still, I suppose I can understand it,
in a way. You were beside yourself—it was a demented
action. But Ben Manning—that was different. You killed
him in cold blood. And it's very possible he never would
have proved as big a threat as you supposed. He was only
trying to find Ted Wood."

She shook her head grimly. "You're wrong, Mr. Kramer.
He was on to this whole affair just as you were. But he made
different deductions than you've made. Because he was a
different kind of man. And he had different intentions."

"Such as?"

"Money."

"On what basis?"

"Someone told him that I had once threatened to kill Dr. Castle. That was true, of course. In a rage, during a quarrel long ago, I had done just that, meaning it then about as much as women usually mean it when they say it in a rage."

"Where had that quarrel taken place?"

"In the driveway at Dr. Castle's home. Late one night when I had gone there, knowing Mrs. Castle would be gone, and waited for David to get home. Another night, you see, when—when my feelings got out of control?"

"How long ago?"

"Perhaps a year before David died."

"Ted Wood was working there then. It must have been he who overheard that quarrel. And he could have told Manning about it, possibly just to get Manning off his own back."

"I don't understand. If Ted Wood is missing—"

"He isn't—not any longer. He's been living nearby under an assumed name and living very well on money he was extorting from Mrs. Castle by making her believe her husband was still alive and had perpetrated an insurance swindle. But he was captured tonight while trying to take Mrs. Castle for another fifty thousand."

She laughed—a small humorless sound.

"What precisely did Manning want of you?" I asked.

"Twenty-five thousand, to keep him from telling the police I had made threats against David's life. You may be right that even if he had carried out his threat nothing would have come of it, since the case had been officially closed as accidental death. But it wasn't a matter on which I could afford to take a chance. While we talked I moved over there to that table, then turned and snatched the gun I kept there in a drawer. Maybe I only intended to scare him off, I'm not sure. But he jumped me and I fired twice and killed him. He was a small man and I'm a big woman. Doing what I did with him was not too difficult."

"Why did you take him up to the Castle property? Did you think that if he were ever found it might tend to implicate Mrs. Castle?"

"Partly. But also because it was an isolated place where I could work safely."

"And Casey?"

"I knew there was a chance you'd decide to check out that typewriter business. I decided that was a chance I couldn't take, either. If I could have gotten that customer slip from him without harming him . . . But he would have remembered me asking for it. There was no other way. It's the one thing I regret."

"So now what, Miss Parker? You'd regret this too, wouldn't you? And it would be futile. Because there's a squad car parked out in front of the house. Lieutenant Foster and another man are waiting for me. If I don't come out in half an hour they come in."

"I see."

She stood very still, her eyes resting on me with a remote expression as if her thoughts were far away. "But I don't think I would have killed you anyway, Mr. Kramer," she said at last. "Do you know why? Because you said you could understand the way I felt—and why I had to do what I did—about David. Perhaps you didn't really, but you said it anyway, and that was a kindness. And when your life has been as empty of love and understanding as mine has been —well, you are grateful for little crumbs like that, you know. Any crumb at all, from anyone at all."

She turned and put the pistol down on the mantelpiece,

then walked away to a distance. I went over and picked it up and pocketed it. Then I went to the front window. I raised the blind and lowered it again—the signal for Foster. When I turned around she was sitting with her large capable hands folded neatly in her lap and her eyes downcast.

"I'm glad it's over," she said. "It's been a long time."

21

LEE PUFFED contentedly at his pipe. "I still don't see why you felt so sure it was Irene Parker. I'd have picked Mrs. Castle."

"If she had ever married Rainier, I might have, too. But here was a woman who, as long as there was the remotest chance of her husband being alive, wasn't risking bigamy. It just seemed to me that anybody that shy of a little thing like bigamy hadn't dabbled in murder."

"I see. And this sister. She just went back to New York without even letting you know."

"Yeah. She apparently figured Ted Wood was in pretty deep and if she kept probing she'd have him behind bars, which she naturally didn't want to do. So she cleared out to discourage further investigation. Of course, she didn't know we already had him in custody."

"She'll probably come back now and try to do something for him though. Hire a good attorney and like that."

"I have an idea she won't. She's not the kind of person who would—uh—countenance his type of activity."

"You mean she'd let her own brother down? Well, what kind of woman is *that?*"

I sighed and rose and walked to the window. "Who ever knows what kind of woman any woman is?"

"Well—" Lee stashed his pipe in the tray and reached for some papers. "Maybe we can get back to normal around here now. No more silly poems in the mail. No more hippies. No more beautiful dames with lost brothers. Maybe we can even get down to business on the Emerson estate."

"Yeah, I guess so. I want to go out and see Rufus Langley, though. I think he deserves to hear the whole story. After all, if it hadn't been for his typewriter we might never have learned the truth."

"In view of how convinced he was that it was Mrs. Castle and Rainier who had killed his brother, what makes you think he'll believe the story?"

"If you can believe you wrote *Gone With the Wind* you can believe anything, can't you?"

There was a tap at the door, and Mickey came in.

"You look funny," I said.

"That's possible," she said with dignity. "But so will you when you hear the latest. I have been on the phone with Mrs. Highland, the Emerson housekeeper."

"So?"

"You aren't going to believe this."

"Believe what?"

"Nightingale Emerson just had kittens."